WHISPERS OF CHANGE

BOOK 39 THE AMISH BONNET SISTERS

SAMANTHA PRICE

FOREWARD

With so many new characters and some visiting older ones, I thought it might be helpful to have a list of who's who.

Character List:
New to the series:
Gabe (Malachi and Jed's older brother)
Wilma's Daughters:
Mercy (married to Stephen)
Honor (married to Jonathon)
Joy (married to Isaac)
Hope (married to Fairfax)
Favor (married to Simon)
Cherish (married to Malachi)
Wilma's stepchildren from her first husband, Josiah:
Earl (married to Miriam)
Mark (married to Christina)
Florence (married to Carter)

Wilma's stepdaughter from her second husband, Levi:

Bliss (married to Adam)

Ada's nephews:

Jonathon (married to Honor)

Stephen (married to Mercy)

Matthew (works in the orchard)

Young women living with Wilma.

Debbie (Levi's niece, has a tea business, and currently lives with Wilma)

Jared (Debbie's young son)

Krystal (dating Jed, and has a quilt store. She is also currently living with Wilma)

Wilma's friends

Ada Berger (Wilma's best friend. She is married to Samuel)

Susan Maine

Daphne Hinkle

Eli Radmacher (A widower, friend of the family)

Other characters:

Ruth (Englisher neighbour of Cherish and Malachi)

Harriet and Melvin (Favor's in-laws)

Fritz White (Engaged to Debbie)

Peter White (Debbie's ex boyfriend and Fritz's brother).

CHAPTER 1

DEBBIE STIRRED the pot of stew simmering on the stove; its aroma filled Wilma's kitchen. She glanced at the calendar on the kitchen wall, the bold red circle around a date growing ever closer.

Only two weeks until she'd be Mrs. Fritz White.

Some things were falling into place, yet there was so much more to be done.

Florence had been working tirelessly on the dresses for the wedding, and Debbie couldn't help but feel a twinge of guilt every time she thought about it. Florence was always ready to help, but with Fritz's suit added at the last minute to Florence's tasks, she hoped it wasn't too much for her with the new baby.

While Fritz had spent little time with Debbie because of the distance between them, their letters and brief visits had helped solidify their bond.

A more immediate concern was on her mind.

Uncle Levi's house.

Debbie felt a deep appreciation for the proposed gift from Aunt Wilma on behalf of Uncle Levi, but Fritz hadn't sounded thrilled.

Debbie's thoughts were interrupted by Aunt Wilma, who was busy pouring flour into a bowl. "Debbie, have you and Fritz discussed where you'll visit after the wedding?"

Debbie looked at her aunt, biting her lip. "I've mentioned meeting his relatives, maybe traveling for a bit... but Fritz doesn't want to do that, especially since he's relocating back here. It's such a big move, he wants to stay put for a while."

Wilma nodded. "It's important for young couples to make their own decisions. But traveling can be a wonderful experience before settling down. I know he's traveled a lot, but you haven't. I hope you get to do that before the babies arrive. That'll make things so much harder."

Before Debbie could reply, Ada bounded in through the back door, a bunch of parsley in her hand. "Are we talking about the wedding again?"

"Yes," Debbie said with a grin. It had been nearly their only topic of conversation in these past weeks. "I just want everything to go perfectly and our marriage to follow the same pattern."

"You two will find your rhythm, Debbie. Remember, every couple has their adjustments. It's only natural," Wilma said.

Ada chuckled. "Adjustments are the fun part. You

get to discover all these quirky habits about each other."

Debbie didn't know if she liked the sound of quirky habits. She had never liked surprises. "Like what?"

Ada giggled. "Well, how Samuel always misplaces his shoes, or how he insists on having his morning coffee exactly at seven. No earlier and no later."

Wilma looked over at Ada. "I didn't know that. That must be hard to get right every morning."

"Well, what adjustment stories do you have to share, Wilma?" Debbie asked.

Wilma thought for a moment. "Levi always used to hum a tune when he was deep in thought, even though he claimed he never did."

They all laughed. "I remember him doing that," Debbie said. "I never knew he denied it."

"Your wedding day is going to be *wunderbaar.* Family and friends will be back here. It's going to be like the good old days," Ada said as she sat at the table to chop the parsley.

"I hope so, but I heard that Earl, Miriam, and their little tribe won't be able to make it."

Ada sighed dramatically. "Well, we'll just have to eat twice as much and have even more fun on their behalf."

"Don't say we'll eat more, Ada. I'll have to get Florence to make my dress bigger." Debbie laughed.

Ada nodded. "I was wondering why the dresses she made me and Wilma were roomy."

With each passing moment, Debbie felt the excitement and anxiety intertwining. But looking at Aunt Wilma and Ada, reminded her of the love and support surrounding her. It meant so much since she was estranged from her parents and from her late husband's family.

"Now, after you two lovebirds tie the knot, all our sights will be set on Krystal's big day. Do you think she's next in line for marriage?" Ada asked.

Debbie grinned at the thought. "We all know that the two of them are meant to be together. It's only a matter of when, not if."

"Everyone knows that except Matthew. But, I think he's given up on winning her back," Wilma said.

"Seems love is in the air. First you, Debbie, then possibly Krystal... Who knows? Maybe it'll be Wilma next." Ada winked, causing both Debbie and Aunt Wilma to laugh.

Debbie placed the lid on the stew. "Well, if that's the case, Florence is going to have her hands full with all these wedding dresses she'll be making."

Ada nodded. "We can give her a hand. After all, it's always merrier when people work together."

Wilma looked around. "Where's Jared?"

"He's on the porch talking with Matthew. They were deep in some discussion when I saw them last," Debbie said.

Ada's face brightened. "What were they talking about, do you know?"

"I'm not sure. I think they were talking about horses."

Ada clucked her tongue. "I wish Matthew could find a lady. Maybe he'll meet someone special at your wedding, Debbie. There's going to be quite a crowd. I've heard from so many friends that are coming from far away."

Debbie thought for a moment. "It's a possibility that he'll meet someone, but don't you think he's got a lot of growing up to do before he's ready?"

Ada frowned at her. "Why do you say that?"

"Well, it was only a few months ago that he was sleeping on the porch, hoping to glimpse Krystal as she passed by or some such thing. Before that, he was trying to court one woman after another, then expecting Krystal to forget what he did."

"You have a point, Debbie," Wilma said. "But maybe a woman will help him mature."

"Anything is possible, but maybe a woman wants a mature man to start with. That's why Fritz is good for me. He's mature."

Ada chuckled as she picked up beans and sliced them into a bowl. "Do you have pre-wedding nerves, Debbie?"

"A bit, I suppose. I don't even know where we'll be living. He said we'll sort that out when he gets here."

Wilma looked up. "Won't you be living in the house I showed you? Carter is getting the transfer organized."

"Yes, I mean, I'm not sure." Debbie was embarrassed by Fritz not working this out before now.

Wilma exhaled a huff. "You need to know where you're going. Didn't he say he wanted to pay for the house? That's not why I offered it to both of you, but I wanted to discuss that with Fritz face-to-face. It's meant to be a gift. I never knew you had decided against moving into it."

"Thanks, Wilma. I really hope we can sort something out soon. I don't want you to think I'm ungrateful because I'm not, neither is Fritz. I'd love to live in that house, but he seems to be unsure."

Ada shook her head. "Why don't you know what's going on? You don't seem to communicate with Fritz very much."

"I do, but he's so busy all the time. I don't like to bother him with anything. He even has less time now with the big move."

"When he gets here, he'll have to give you some answers," Ada said with a nod. "Time's running out like the sand through an hourglass. Time won't wait for him to decide, it just keeps moving."

"That'll be the first thing we'll need to clear up when he gets here."

Wilma stared up at the ceiling, lost in thought. "I can't wait until I have all my girls under one roof again. Just think, in a few days, they'll all be here."

"It'll be noisy, I know that much." After Ada placed the green vegetables into boiling water, she busied herself with making a pot of tea.

Debbie couldn't help but wonder what her life would be like once she was married. She had always dreamed of a happy home filled with love. But how close would real life measure up to her imaginings?

CHAPTER 2

OUT ON THE PORCH, Jared sat patiently with Matthew beside him. They were both on standby to assist Krystal with her horse the moment she arrived home.

"Are you sure Jed won't be coming here this afternoon?" Matthew asked.

"Yeah. That's what I heard."

Matthew looked down at the young boy, feeling a twinge of guilt that he was just sitting there with Jared when he could've been off playing somewhere. "You don't have to wait here with me."

"I want to."

"Well, I'll do something that you want. Shall we kick a ball around while we wait? Or maybe do something else?"

Jared tilted his head thoughtfully, his bright blue eyes reflecting determination. "I've been wanting to improve my handwriting."

Raising an eyebrow, Matthew responded, "I thought you were already one of the top students."

Jared's small face scrunched up. "I'm good at some stuff, but there are some kids who write better."

Matthew leaned closer. "You know that many of the kids in your class are older, right? They've had years more practice."

"Doesn't matter. I want to be better."

Chuckling softly, Matthew patted Jared's head. "Alright then, let's see what you've got."

Jared eagerly pulled out a notebook and pencil from his small bag, scribbling a few words. Matthew observed, noticing the clumsy grip and erratic movements.

"Wait a minute," Matthew said. "You're doing it all wrong." He adjusted the way Jared held his pencil. "This will give you better control."

"Are you sure?" Jared looked up at him.

"Try it."

Jared wrote again, producing marginally better strokes. "That's a bit better already. Thanks, Matthew."

"Better, yeah?" Matthew asked.

"Yeah. Show me more."

"It's nice to be appreciated. Good to know I'm good at something."

Over the next several minutes, the two of them were engrossed. Matthew demonstrated the fluid motion of writing letters, explaining the curves and the lines. Then Jared would try to replicate what he wrote.

After several trials, Jared's face lit up with a

mischievous idea. "Can you write a note to someone, and then I'll copy it?"

Matthew chuckled. "Sure thing. What would you like me to write?"

Grinning, Jared proposed, "How about... Jared should not eat his vegetables tonight. It's important. From Ada."

The sheer audacity of the note caught Matthew off guard, and he burst into laughter. "You little rascal! Where do you come up with these things?" Yet, he couldn't resist and proceeded to write the note in his best handwriting.

Jared tried copying, his tongue between his teeth in concentration. The result was a jumbled mix of shaky letters, some oversized and others barely visible.

"Mine's not as good. Can I keep yours so I can keep trying?"

"Sure. You can't use the note, okay?" Matthew said.

Jared shook his head. "It's just for us. No one will know about it."

"Throw it out when you're done."

The duo continued their fun activity, with Jared suggesting more dramatic and hilarious notes. From declaring a ban on broccoli to officially resigning from chores, they crafted an array of declarations.

Matthew steered the conversation to a slightly more personal territory. "How's Krystal doing?" he asked, his voice filled with genuine concern.

Jared paused in his writing, his gaze drifting

momentarily. "She's okay," he responded, scribbling a bit more forcefully on the paper.

Matthew noted the change in Jared's demeanor. "And what about Jed? Any sign of him going home?"

Jared's grip on his pencil tightened momentarily. "No," he said, trying to sound casual, but the weight of the subject was evident in his voice. "I don't think he's going back."

Silence settled between them for a few moments. Matthew broke the quietness. "There's a rumor going around."

"What is it?" Jared asked.

"I heard you might be getting a new dad soon," Matthew said playfully.

Jared's face brightened immediately; the cloud of sadness replaced by childlike enthusiasm. "Yeah!"

"That sounds exciting. And a new house, too?"

Jared's exuberance faded slightly. "Yeah... but I haven't seen it. I'm a bit worried."

Matthew tilted his head, trying to decipher the boy's sudden melancholy. "You're too young to worry. You have to wait until you are at least my age for that. What's troubling you?"

Jared bit his lip, his gaze falling to his half-written notes. "It's just... I don't want to leave behind the birdhouse that Eli and Wilma helped me make. Birds come there every day now. It's their home."

Matthew nodded, trying to hold back his laughter. If only his worries were so small. "Why not take it with you?"

Jared's face scrunched up in thought. "But the birds... they're used to sheltering in there now. What will they do without it?"

"Hmm. Let's think about that. You know, birds are adaptable. They'll find another place. But if it worries you so much, why not make another one? An identical one. Leave one here for the birds you've grown attached to, and take the other with you."

Jared's eyes lit up. "Great idea."

Matthew chuckled. "Want some help? Time's running out today, but I can come back tomorrow afternoon."

Jared's face broke into a broad grin. "No. I know someone that can help me make another one."

Matthew tapped his chin. "Let's see now, would that be Eli?"

Jared laughed. "Yes."

"Okay. I don't mind. I'll just stick to helping you with writing."

Jared looked down at the paper. "You're doing a good job at that."

Matthew grinned. "Thank you. As I said, nice to know I'm useful for something." Matthew bounded to his feet when he saw a horse and buggy heading to the house.

Then Jared looked over at the approaching horse and buggy and got to his feet. "Oh no. Isn't that Jed driving the buggy?"

Matthew gritted his teeth. "Yeah. Looks like it. I thought you said he wouldn't be here tonight."

"Sorry, Matthew. I got it wrong."

Matthew put a hand on Jared's shoulder. "It's okay, kid. You did your best. I'm gonna get out of here before they see me."

Jared watched Matthew head to the end of the porch and jump over the railing.

CHAPTER 3

CHERISH, hearing the rumble of a car, stepped out onto the porch, her eyes lighting up when she saw Ruth. "Hi," she called out, hurrying down the steps.

Ruth stepped out of the vehicle, her face creased with concern. "Hi, Cherish. Have you heard anything from Jed?"

"Last I heard, he's fallen in love with Krystal and has even started a touring business there so he can stay."

"Hmm. I had hoped he would find his way back here. I kind of got used to him being around," she admitted, her voice catching slightly.

Cherish placed a comforting hand on Ruth's arm. "I don't know if he'll be coming back at all."

"I see. It's so quiet without him. He was good company."

Seeing Ruth's downcast expression, Cherish quickly thought of a way to cheer her up, "Why don't you come with us to Debbie's wedding? Jed will be there. It might be good for both of you to reconnect."

Ruth's eyes brightened at the prospect. "Your family wouldn't mind?"

"Of course not. My mother and Ada will be so happy to see you again."

Ruth hesitated for a moment before admitting, "I do miss him, you know."

"I know. And he thinks the world of you, too. This would be a perfect opportunity for you two to see each other again."

After a moment of contemplation, Ruth's face lit up with resolve. "Alright, I'll do it. I'll come with you to the wedding. And... I can even drive you if you'd like."

Cherish clapped her hands together. "That would be wonderful. Thank you. Malachi won't be going, but Favor will probably want to come, too, if she's well enough."

Ruth chuckled. "The more, the merrier, right? It'll be like a road trip. We'll have a great time."

"I can't wait. I'm going over to tell Favor right now. Oh, unless you'd like to come in and have coffee?"

Ruth shook her head. "No. I'm on my way to the store. Why don't you stop by after you speak with Favor. I'll buy us a cake."

Cherish was delighted that she was buying the cake rather than trying to make it. She was the worst cook ever. "Thanks, Ruth. I'll do that."

CHAPTER 4

FAVOR LOUNGED on the couch by the window, dramatically clutching her midriff, feigning the discomfort of morning sickness. She sighed loudly to the sounds of Harriet working tirelessly in the kitchen. The tantalizing aroma of freshly baked bread wafted in, making Favor's mouth water. *Perhaps a small slice won't hurt,* she mused.

As she considered her excuse to Harriet for suddenly being hungry, she heard a horse and buggy. She looked outside to see Cherish.

Favor could always count on her sister for some light-hearted gossip or a fun distraction from her pretend ailments.

Two seconds later, Cherish burst into the house and stood in front of Favor. "You wouldn't believe the news I have."

Favor sat upright. "You're having a baby?"

"No, silly." Cherish sat beside Favor and continued,

"Ruth has offered to drive us to Debbie's wedding. Isn't that just perfect?"

The idea of traveling with Ruth was enticing; it promised a change from the usual monotony of traveling in hired cars. "That sounds wonderful! I love Ruth. When do we leave?"

"In two days," Cherish chirped, clasping her hands together. "Oh, I forgot to tell Ruth when we were leaving. She's invited me to her place when I finish here so I'll tell her then. Are you well enough to come with me to Ruth's?"

Favor leaned forward and whispered, "I can't. Harriet thinks I've still got morning sickness."

Cherish's head tilted to one side. "Why would she think that?"

Favor looked away.

"Oh, you're dreadful. Are you doing that so Harriet will do everything?"

"Kind of." When Cherish shook her head, Favor added, "I am a little more tired than usual. Anyway, I can't wait! It'll be such an adventure. I'm looking forward to seeing everyone again. I've missed *Mamm* so much."

"I think Ruth's only going so she can check up on Jed. She's like a mother hen." Cherish chuckled.

Harriet, having overheard part of their exchange, entered the room, her hands on her hips. "Favor, do you really think you'll be well enough to go to Debbie's wedding?"

"Ah, well, the morning sickness comes and goes."

"Not lately, you've had it consistently these past months. I don't know if going to the wedding is a good idea."

"Harriet, she can't miss this. Debbie is like one of our sisters almost," Cherish said. "She'll have to drag herself there no matter how many stops we'll need to make along the way."

Harriet's lips turned down at the corners as she turned from Cherish to Favor. "Last I checked this morning, you could barely lift your head from the couch. Funny, you're looking better already."

Favor paled, realizing her ruse might have just cost her a delightful journey. She stammered, "B...but Harriet, I've been feeling much better lately. I've improved. Really."

Cherish, sensing the tension, tried to mediate. "Perhaps the trip might do her some good, Harriet. A change of scenery could help."

"No. If Favor is well enough to travel, she's well enough to stay here and work."

Favor's heart sank. In a last-ditch effort, she protested, "It's Debbie's wedding. I must be there. No matter how sick I am, I've gotta be at her wedding."

Harriet looked at Favor. "Hmm, it makes me wonder."

"What? Wait, do you think I'm not really feeling ill? I am pregnant and…"

"I'm sorry, Favor, but I can't allow you to go. Simon would also agree, and I know you wouldn't go against what he wants. You are carrying his child, after all."

Favor's eyes grew wide. She immediately regretted exaggerating her symptoms. "Please, Ma. Let me go?"

"Well, there is one way I'll let you go."

Favor grinned and looked over at Cherish and then back to Harriet. "What is it?"

"The only way I'll let you go is if I come too."

Favor was disappointed. Now, she'd have to keep pretending she wasn't well.

"That would be wonderful. I don't know why I didn't think of it. It's a big car, and I'm sure Ruth won't mind. This way, Favor can attend the wedding, and Harriet, you get a well-deserved break. Plus, Mamm and Ada would love to have you there."

Favor had no choice but to agree with Cherish. She nodded vigorously. "Would you do that, Ma? Cherish is right. And, aren't you like Ada's second best friend or something?"

Harriet chuckled. After a long pause, she said, "Alright, we'll all go. But Favor, when we return, I expect you to step up and help more."

Favor, relief flooding her, got up and hugged Harriet tightly. "I will, if I'm feeling better by then."

"The men can stay here and work." Harriet grinned. "There's no need for them to go."

"Oh yes." Cherish agreed. "Malachi already said he'd stay behind, and every spare moment, he'll be over here helping Melvin and Simon."

"It's settled then," Harriet said with a nod. "Two days, you say?"

"Yes. We're leaving on Thursday, and we'll be

staying for a few days after the wedding," Cherish said as she glanced back at Favor.

Favor smiled, but now she had to stop acting so helpless.

"Just imagine the fun we'll have on the road. And think about the stories we can share when we return. Ruth's car is spacious and so comfortable," Cherish said.

Harriet, though a tad more reserved than Cherish, couldn't help but share in the excitement. "It's been ages since I've attended a wedding. And even though I don't know Debbie well, I know she's had a rough time. It'll be a joy to see her happy and settled."

Favor, lost in thought, barely noticed when Cherish nudged her gently. "Hey, what are you going to wear?"

"Ah," Favor responded, a little startled. "I'll wear my Sunday best. I guess I'll have to start making bigger clothes."

"No. You can get some from Joy or Christina. They'll have some maternity dresses left over. They won't mind if you borrow them, I'm sure."

"Good idea. I hope the travel doesn't worsen my morning sickness."

Harriet's eyes filled with concern. "I know how difficult it's been for you lately. We can always make more stops if you feel sick. And I'll pack some ginger tea. I know how you like that."

Cherish, sensing the shift in mood, tried to lighten the atmosphere. "We'll take care of you. Think of all the pampering you'll get at the wedding."

They all chuckled, but Favor felt a twinge of guilt. "Thank you, both of you. It means a lot to me that you're so understanding of how I'm feeling. Being pregnant is not an illness, but sometimes it sure feels like it."

Harriet leaned in, placing a comforting hand on Favor's. "Child, that's what family does. We support each other through thick and thin. This journey is not just about attending a wedding. It's about being together, creating memories."

Cherish nodded. "And if Ruth is driving, we'll have even more stories to tell. Do you remember that time she mistook the brake for the accelerator?"

Harriet drew back, horrified. "What?"

Cherish covered her mouth and giggled. "I'm only joking. Don't worry. She's safe at driving, Harriet, but she's not safe at cooking. Speaking of that, I must go." Cherish got to her feet and headed out the door, leaving Harriet and Favor looking at each other.

Harriet's eyebrows rose. "What did she mean by that?"

Favor shook her head. "I'm not sure. Do you think you could make me a sandwich?"

CHAPTER 5

WILMA STIRRED her tea at the bi-weekly get-together with her friends. Debbie and Ada flanked her on one side, and across from her sat Susan Maine and Daphne Hinkle. In the midst of the chatter, she was lost in thoughts of the upcoming wedding and the logistics of who would stay where. Figuring it all out was proving to be quite the challenge.

Ada sensed her concern, and when there was a lull in the conversation, she said, "You've got that worried look, Wilma. Speak your mind. What's going on?"

Wilma sighed, placing her teacup down on the saucer. "It's not the wedding itself. It's where everyone will stay. That's my main concern right now. With Mercy, Honor, and their families coming, I don't know how I'll fit everyone in. This is a big house, so it can be done, but then I'll have the job of cleaning around everyone and trying to cook for the wedding while also feeding the guests."

Ada leaned back in her chair. "Well, I can host some of them if it helps. My home is always open, you know that. I have Jed there, but he can move to the attic. There's a bed up there. I'm sure he won't mind."

"That might be the answer. I have so much going on with the wedding, and Mercy and Honor are coming with their young children..."

"Say no more," Ada replied with a wave of her hand. "Of course, I'll take them in. They're family, after all. It's nearly the same, not my family, but your family."

Susan pushed her glasses higher on her nose. "I am already hosting some relatives who are coming to Debbie's wedding."

"Me as well," Daphne said. "I will have a full house. Otherwise, I would've offered."

Wilma smiled at both friends. "I appreciate that." Then she turned to Ada. "What do you need to prepare your home? I mean, with Mercy and Honor's four boys... they can be quite the handful. Do you have enough bedding? Toys to keep them occupied if it rains? They might be staying for more than a week."

Ada waved her concerns away. "Don't you worry about that. I still have some board games from when my children were young. And as for bedding, I've got plenty. But perhaps we could plan some activities for the children? Maybe a little crafting session or a day out in the fields? Perhaps Jed can take them on one of his tours." Ada chuckled.

Wilma's eyes lit up at the idea. "I could organize

some supplies for crafting. Maybe they could make something special for the wedding."

Daphne suggested, "How about we help them make decorative pieces for the tables? It'll make them feel involved and excited about the wedding."

"I love that idea," Susan said, and then added, "Ada, did you make any more of that delicious red velvet cake?"

"No, Susan, we're finished with testing the cakes. You'll get to eat as much cake as you want at the wedding, including the red velvet cakes I'll be making." Ada leaned forward and slid the plate of cookies further along the table toward her. "For now, all we have are cookies."

Susan took a cookie off the plate. "I do like weddings and cake." Susan nibbled on the cookie.

Ada narrowed her eyes at Susan and then continued where the conversation had left off, "Yes, Daphne, something to make the children feel involved. Children often feel pushed to one side. That's what I've learned from speaking with Jared. That boy always says how he feels."

Debbie nodded. "It's hard being an only child. I would've loved to have had a sibling. I was around adults a lot too."

Wilma thought about that for a moment. "Now you mention it, Ada, what if Mercy and Honor feel pushed aside when I ask them to stay with you? I don't want them to feel... unwelcome in their own family home."

Ada chuckled. "Oh, they've grown up, Wilma.

They're not the same self-centered girls they used to be. I'm sure they'll understand. Besides, a change of scenery might be fun for them. They haven't stayed at my place since they were children."

Wilma gave a relieved sigh. "Thank you. Cherish and Favor are coming without their husbands, so they can take the two spare bedrooms here. I do need to look after Favor now that she's expecting." Wilma tapped her finger on the rim of her cup, her mind turning over. "I just hope it doesn't create division or jealousy amongst the girls. I love all of them dearly. The last thing I want is for them to feel less than one or both of their sisters."

Debbie placed a comforting hand on Wilma's shoulder. "Everyone understands how much is going on with the wedding. And with Mercy and Honor's young boys, it might be best to be at Ada's, where they can play and not be underfoot as we prepare. We'll be cleaning, cooking, and all that for days before the big day."

Wilma nodded slowly. "I know, you're right. I must trust that everyone will understand and that things will go smoothly. Of course, they'll be over here a lot, and they'd love to play with Jared, too."

"That's right. They'll visit, but they'll be staying with Ada. It sounds perfect," Debbie said.

"And Jared can always have a sleepover with his cousins if he wants."

"Thanks, Ada. They aren't cousins, but I suppose we

can call them that. I'm sure he'll love spending time with them."

Wilma's fingers nervously twiddled with her napkin, reflecting on the emotions the upcoming event was stirring within her. It wasn't just about lodging; it was the emotional dynamics, the memories of raising her girls, and ensuring everyone felt equal attention.

Seeing Wilma's worried face, Debbie said, "Don't overthink things, Aunt Wilma. Everyone's coming together for something happy. People are always happy at weddings."

Wilma smiled faintly, "You're wise beyond your years, Debbie. It's just that, as a mother, I want every-thing to be perfect for everyone. Mercy and Honor live so far away now that I don't want them to feel pushed aside when they get here. And I don't want them feeling I'm playing favorites."

Susan wasn't really listening to the conversation. "So, besides red velvet, what other cakes are we having at your wedding, Debbie?"

Debbie's face lit up. "Oh, there will be so many cakes. Wilma, Ada, and I are making several of them, and I'm also buying a lot from a local bakery."

"Hungry are we?" Ada asked Susan.

"No. I just like cakes."

Ada looked back at Wilma. "Wilma, I've known those girls since they were babies. They've matured into fine young women. Remember that big quarrel Mercy and Honor had over that one doll? They've come a long way since. Where they're staying won't bother them one bit."

"Maybe we could organize a pre-wedding family dinner," Debbie suggested. "To ensure everyone's on the same page, and it's clear that all decisions are made out of love and necessity."

Wilma's face brightened. "Yes, we'll be doing plenty of those. It'll be so lovely to have everyone here again."

Ada nodded approvingly. "If there are any issues, you can explain your thoughts during dinner. Face-to-face conversations always work best."

Wilma hoped it would be as easy as everyone thought. "Thank you, everyone. In times like these, I realize how blessed I am to have such supportive friends."

Debbie put an arm around her aunt's shoulders. "It's going to be a beautiful wedding, and every moment leading up to it should be filled with happiness. Let's not borrow troubles from tomorrow."

"Ah, that's a good thought. *Denke* for the reminder. I tend to worry too much. I'll leave things in *Gott's* hands."

CHAPTER 6

THAT NIGHT, it was just Wilma, Debbie, Krystal, and Jared for dinner. Wilma was still buzzing with excitement about the return of four of her daughters who lived far away. She was quickly moving around the kitchen, preparing salad and keeping an eye on the pasta and leftover chicken.

Debbie set the table while Krystal sat, listening to Wilma's energetic chatter. Jared played with small wooden horses, imitating their neighing sounds and occasionally giggling at something amusing in his own little world.

"You know," Wilma began, her voice dripping with excitement, "it's been ages since all my girls were under one roof. And with the wedding, everyone's coming back. I can't even say how much it means to me."

Krystal added, "It'll be like those old days when we'd sleep in each other's rooms, braid each other's hair, and sneak into the kitchen for midnight snacks."

Wilma chuckled. "I remember those nights. I'd pretend not to notice the next morning—missing cookies or the telltale crumbs on the counter."

Wilma stumbled upon a folded piece of paper in the middle of the table. Opening it, she squinted at the neat handwriting.

"What's that, Wilma?" Debbie asked.

"It's a note from Ada. That's odd. I wonder why she left a note. She was just here."

Debbie looked over her shoulder. "What does it say?"

Wilma's eyebrows furrowed in confusion. "It says 'make sure Jared doesn't eat any vegetables tonight.'"

Debbie went back to setting the table. "Why would Ada say something like that?"

Wilma shook her head, equally perplexed. "She was over earlier, chatting about the upcoming wedding, but she mentioned nothing about vegetables or Jared."

Jared looked up and then went back to innocently playing with his horses.

Debbie caught his expression. "Jared, do you know anything about this?"

Jared shook his head. "Me? I've already eaten enough vegetables to make me strong. Maybe she thinks I'm strong enough."

Debbie looked back at Wilma. "It is odd, but you know how Ada is fussy about food."

Krystal added, "But if there was something wrong with the vegetables, she would've said for all of us not to eat them."

Wilma sighed, placing the note down on the table. "We'll have to ask her tomorrow. For now, let's just do what she says. It's just one evening, and we aren't having many vegetables tonight."

"Okay," Debbie agreed. "One night without them won't hurt him."

That evening, Jared enjoyed a dinner free of vegetables, much to his delight. Jared chuckled to himself, already thinking about the next mischief he could cook up with Matthew's notes.

CHAPTER 7

THE FOLLOWING MORNING, Ada arrived, and as she sat with Wilma enjoying a crackling fire and their hot tea, Wilma brought up the note she'd found.

"Ada," she began, "I found the note you left regarding Jared not eating any vegetables. I followed it, but I'm curious to know what was wrong with Jared eating the vegetables. None of us had any last night just in case something was badly wrong with them."

Ada's eyebrows pinched together. "What was that, Wilma?"

"Why did you leave the note about vegetables?"

Ada put her teacup down on the saucer and stared at Wilma. "I didn't leave any note about vegetables."

"Your note said that Jared wasn't to eat any vegetables."

"What?" Ada shook her head. "I never did such a thing. No. I'd say Jared might've written it himself."

"No, he couldn't have. The writing was too good," Wilma insisted.

"*Jah,* it must've been good if you thought it was my handwriting. Do you still have the note, Wilma?"

"I kept it." Wilma headed into the kitchen to get it.

She returned a moment later, holding the small piece of paper. Ada took it and studied it closely. "This looks a bit like mine, but not quite," she remarked as her lips turned down. "Someone tried to imitate my writing, it seems. The loops on the 'h' and the curve on the 'y' are slightly off."

Wilma bit her lip, wondering who could've done such a thing. "This is wrong. No one should sign it with your name. But Jared's played his little tricks now and then. I see him feeding Red some of his meal when he thinks no one's looking, but would he really do this?"

Ada slowly nodded. "It could only have been him. Ah, that boy! Always up to something. But avoiding vegetables? That's quite a leap."

"I know. Debbie's got enough to worry about, so I'll talk with him about it as soon as he gets home from school."

"Wilma, I think we should play a little trick on Jared in return."

Wilma grinned. "I like the sound of that. What do you have in mind?"

"You remember the zucchini bread recipe I shared with you last week?" Ada's eyes gleamed with mischief.

Wilma grinned. "Oh, I see where you're going with this."

For the rest of the day, the two women worked diligently in the kitchen, occasionally breaking into fits of giggles. By the afternoon, they had prepared a feast, and every dish had a twist. They had zucchini bread, carrot cake, potato chocolate chip cookies, and spinach brownies. Even the lemonade had a dash of cucumber juice.

CHAPTER 8

LATER, when Jared returned from school, Wilma was waiting for him in the living room, her posture stiff, ready for a serious talk.

Ada directed him to sit down in front of Wilma and then Ada disappeared into the kitchen.

"Jared," Wilma began sternly, "did you have anything to do with the note from 'Ada' yesterday?"

Jared hesitated, his eyes darting away guiltily. "Well, I may have..."

Wilma cut him off. "Pranks like this might seem fun to you, but they have consequences. Your mother is already under a lot of stress with the wedding preparations. We don't need to give her additional worries, especially ones based on falsehoods."

"What's falsehoods?" Jared asked.

"Things that aren't true."

Jared looked down at his shoes.

"And Fritz," Wilma continued, "he's about to

35

become a part of your family. Would he appreciate hearing about such antics right before his wedding? He expects to join a household that's harmonious and respectful. Don't you want your mother and Fritz to be happy?"

Jared nodded slowly. "I'm sorry, Aunt Wilma. I won't do it again."

Wilma sighed, her stern expression softening slightly. She'd always had a soft spot for Jared. "I understand wanting to have fun, but it's essential to think about how our actions affect those around us. Especially now, with so many changes happening. Your mother's wedding is a very special thing for her, for both of you. We all want her to be happy, don't we?"

"Yes, Aunt Wilma. I won't do it again. At least not until a long time after the wedding."

Wilma smiled faintly. "That's all I ask for, dear. Let's make sure the next few weeks are filled with joy and celebration, not unnecessary drama. Now, Ada has something very special for you in the kitchen."

"Chocolate cake?" he asked hopefully.

"You'll have to wait and see."

Ada walked out of the kitchen. "Jared, come in here and have a cookie."

He looked over at Wilma, and she gave him a nod. He hurried to the kitchen, and seeing the plate of cookies, he eagerly picked one up and bit into it. He was surprised when he tasted the floury texture and the hint of potato. He swallowed his mouthful. "It's not very nice." Red came up behind him, and Jared lowered his hand, and Red politely took it.

Ada pretended not to notice. "Try a brownie." Ada placed a plate full in front of him.

He tried the brownie next and almost spat it out when he detected the taste of spinach. "Sorry, but this is even worse."

Ada couldn't stop laughing and told Jared that they were going to sneak vegetables into all his meals today.

"And possibly for the next few days," Wilma added.

Jared's face turned a shade of beet-red. Beets—another vegetable he wasn't fond of. "Into everything?"

"Always eat your vegetables, or they'll get back at you. Maybe you'd like the carrot cake?" Ada asked.

Jared made a face. "Carrots in cakes?"

"Yes, try it," Ada urged.

Jared groaned dramatically, picked up a slice of carrot cake, and took a tiny bite. When he swallowed, his face brightened. "Hey, this is good."

The women laughed as Jared took another bite.

After finishing his meal, he went to the barn to start his chores.

As soon as Debbie came home, they told her what they'd found out. She couldn't believe he'd written that note.

CHAPTER 9

THE FOLLOWING DAY, Debbie had another day off from her tea business. Bliss was helping her out, and Krystal was overseeing the packaging and distribution part of the tea business.

Debbie was grateful to have some time to focus on the wedding and becoming a wife.

Although she had been married briefly to Jared's father, she had never experienced a proper marriage, living in the same home as her husband. The brief wedding to John had been a secret and had remained that way until after his death.

Time at home meant more time with Wilma and Ada, and today, they had their mind set on gossip.

As Wilma peered out the window, she asked, "Debbie, would you mind talking with Gabe for us?"

"We're curious about his plans. How long will he stay around here?"

Debbie had no idea why they wanted her to ask

him. She'd stayed home to relax, not to ask people questions. "Ada, he's staying with the bishop. Couldn't you have asked Hannah? She's one of your good friends. Surely Gabe talks with them over dinner or something?"

Ada's eyes twinkled. "I tried, and all she said is that she and the bishop have told Gabe that he's welcome to stay as long as he wants. Everyone's taken quite a liking to him, and we know they have enough room in that big house they've just moved into."

Debbie felt the weight of both sets of eyes on her. "Why do I have to do all these things?"

Wilma and Ada exchanged a glance. "We see how well you get along with him, so we know he'll be more open with you."

Debbie sighed. "Okay, I'll do it, but only because I'll feel bad if I don't."

Ada grinned. "Thank you. Now, we don't want him to know the question is coming from us. We'd love him to stay, and I'd invite him to stay with Samuel and me, but we already have Jed there. There seems to be still some issues between the two brothers, but best not to ask him about that just yet."

"That's right," Wilma added. "We just want to know if he's staying and if he tells you more, it would be great."

Debbie sighed. "What do you mean by more?"

"Well, if he's happy or unhappy with his brother's relationship with Krystal. And if you can find out what his problem is with Jed, that would be good too," Wilma said.

"Good idea, Wilma."

Wilma beamed a smile back at Ada.

Ada got to her feet. "It's a chilly day. I'll make him a hot chocolate to warm him up. I'm sure he'd appreciate it."

"All right, and then after this, can I just do nothing for half an hour? It's such a lovely day, and I just want to daydream about the wedding."

Ada and Wilma both chuckled. "Of course you can," Wilma said.

Ada made the hot drink, and then Debbie headed out into the orchard. When she was halfway there, she turned around and saw Wilma and Ada at the kitchen window, staring. Wilma gave her a little wave while Ada shooed her onward with her hands.

"Oh dear," Wilma sighed. "Why isn't she marrying someone like Gabe? That would be my choice for her."

"I agree. Somehow, I've never felt close to Fritz, but she likes him and that's what truly matters. And he's good with Jared," Ada added.

Wilma agreed but added, "So are other people. Everyone loves Jared."

Ada and Wilma continued to stare out the window.

As Debbie got closer to Gabe, she noticed his shirt sticking to his back, his arms toned and tanned from manual labor. "Hey," she called out, offering a small smile.

Gabe looked up, shielding his eyes from the winter

sun. A slow smile spread across his face. "Hey, Deb." He stood up and brushed the dirt off his hands.

"Thought you might need this." She handed him the mug of hot chocolate.

"Thanks." Gabe took it from her and had a sip. "Nice." He wiped his mouth with the back of his hand and then got dirt all over his chin.

Debbie laughed.

"What's funny?"

She wanted to lean forward and brush the dirt away, but she held back. "You've got dirt on your face now."

"Oh." He laughed and tried to brush it off. "Better?"

"A little."

An awkward silence ensued. Debbie took a deep breath, finally voicing the question everyone had been tiptoeing around. "Gabe, what are your plans? How long do you see yourself here?"

He looked over at the apple trees before he responded. "Truth be told, I'm not sure. I needed a break, Deb. A break from the farm, from my parents, from... everything. Why do you ask?"

"Some of us were wondering, that's all."

Gabe looked over her shoulder at Wilma's house and then smiled when he looked back at Debbie. "I see where this question is coming from."

"You're always welcome here, you know that."

"I know," Gabe replied, his voice soft. "And I'm grateful that the bishop and Hannah have been so hospitable. I'm thinking I might stay on for a while, at least until I figure out what I'm doing. At home, they've got enough workers, and as time goes on, my father won't be able to work and..."

"And there's not enough work for all of your brothers?" Debbie asked.

"Exactly. They'll have to branch out onto their own farms." He handed her back the glass. "Thanks so much. So, are you looking forward to your wedding?"

"I am."

"How do you know, Deb?"

She stared at him. "Know what?"

"If you've got the right person? How can a person be sure?"

Debbie hesitated for a moment, her eyes darting away from Gabe's intense gaze. "I just.. I just know. It's hard to explain."

Gabe nodded slowly. "Yeah, I get it. I'm happy for you."

Debbie smiled. "Thanks, Gabe. I'm happy too. It was a long time coming."

They stood there in comfortable silence for a few moments, watching the apple trees sway gently in the breeze. Then Gabe spoke up again. "Can I ask another question?"

"Sure. Go ahead."

"What would happen if you met someone else before you married him? Someone you liked more."

Debbie laughed. "That wouldn't happen because I wouldn't be looking. I mean, I'm not looking now."

"I'm sorry, I shouldn't have said anything. I admire

anyone who can take a tremendous leap without knowing what's on the other side. I've heard people change after marriage, so… the whole thing is a mystery."

Debbie smiled. "Change for the better, maybe."

Gabe nodded. "Let's hope so."

As they continued to stand by the apple trees, a sudden gust of wind blew past them, sending Debbie's *kapp* strings across her face. Gabe reached out to move them away, his fingers lingering for just a moment longer than necessary.

Gabe cleared his throat and took a step back. "Sorry about that," he said.

"It's okay. It was just the wind."

"You know," Gabe began, looking for the right words. "I've been thinking a lot lately, and I understand that life's complicated. Sometimes, our hearts and minds pull us in different directions. And every decision we make, every turn we take, has its consequences. Some of these consequences cannot be undone and last a lifetime.

Debbie giggled nervously. She hadn't expected such a deep conversation, which, she figured, could only be about marriage. There weren't many decisions besides marriage that couldn't be undone. But he was opening up, so she opened up as well. "I know that more than anyone. I've made my mistakes. I trusted the wrong person. People have let me down."

"I think we all have made mistakes, but that makes us wary about making the next move."

Debbie took a deep breath, her fingers subconsciously playing with the edge of her apron. "That is true, but we can't be too wary. We must trust people again."

Gabe looked away for a moment, collecting his thoughts. When he met her eyes again, his gaze was unwavering. "I've enjoyed our time together over these past months. Your laughter, our conversations... They've meant a lot to me. Everyone here has been so nice."

Debbie felt a lump forming in her throat. She had sensed the underlying connection, but hearing him voice it made it all too real.

"Thanks for the hot chocolate."

"You're welcome."

He put up his arm and leaned against a tree. "When did you meet Fritz?"

"About eighteen months ago."

"Hmm." The wind swept through the trees again, rustling the leaves.

"Why do you ask?"

"No reason in particular. You're not working today?"

"I'm having a couple of days off. Bliss is working for me. I should get back to helping Wilma and Ada."

"Sure. Thanks again, Deb."

Debbie walked away with a spring in her step.

When she walked back into the kitchen, all eyes were on her, waiting for her to speak.

45

CHAPTER 10

"Well, what did he say?" Ada asked.

Debbie placed the mug in the sink and then took a moment to collect her thoughts before speaking. The familiar kitchen felt heavy and stifling after being in the fresh air.

"He's staying longer because he needs a break from things at his farm and his family. He said he likes the orchard work and the company here."

Ada, always quick to sense underlying emotions, narrowed her eyes. "But there's more to it, isn't there? Why can't you look at us right now?"

Debbie sighed, her shoulders sagging a little. "No, nothing."

"I knew it. Didn't I say it, Wilma?"

Wilma stared at Ada. "She didn't say she likes him. Do you, Debbie? Are we calling off the wedding? It's not too late. It's never too late."

Debbie looked from one to the other. "Why would you say such a thing?"

Ada sighed. "I admit we didn't like Fritz at first, but we got a bad first impression of him, didn't we, Wilma?"

"That's right. It's all under the bridge now. Water off a duck's back and all that."

Ada nodded. "Still waters run deep, don't forget that."

Debbie was frustrated with both of them. "Please don't say anything about calling off the wedding. It's a bad omen."

"You're right. I'm sorry," Ada said, looking down.

Debbie gave Ada a nod and then looked at Wilma, waiting for her apology.

"Me too. All we want is for you to be happy."

"And I will be. I am."

Ada nodded slightly. "You and Gabe are just good friends, and there's nothing wrong with that."

Debbie nodded, her fingers tracing the patterns on the tablecloth. Wilma and Ada were trying to make out there was something going on between her and Gabe.

She didn't understand their motivation, but she wished they'd stop. Now, she wished she'd gone to work. "Yes, we get along, and Jared is fond of him. He's become a good friend, just like he is to all of us now. He's no more of a friend to me than he is to anyone else." Debbie put her head in her hands.

Ada and Wilma exchanged a look. "What's wrong now?" Ada asked.

"This is how rumors start. I don't want Fritz to think I am looking at any other man. He's insecure to start with because I was dating his brother."

"No." Ada shook her head. "That's ancient history. And I'm glad we don't have to change any plans. I can't remember the last time a wedding was called off." Ada tapped her chin, looking at the ceiling.

"Please don't even talk about anything like that, Ada. Fritz will be here in a few days. I don't want him to think there are any threats around. I just said that, and you're talking about it again. I want to be happy, not worry about everyone's thoughts."

"I meant nothing by it. I just meant that—"

"She won't talk about it again, will you, Ada?" Wilma asked, staring at her friend.

"I won't if everyone's going to be so upset."

"Thank you," Debbie said.

Ada lifted her head and held back her shoulders. "Now, how about some of that apple pie Wilma just baked? A slice of that, and the world will seem a better place where all decisions are final, just like your wedding vows will be."

"Debbie's not scared by the finality of wedding vows, are you?" Wilma asked.

"No. The finality of them comforts me. If Fritz and I have any issues, we'll just talk about them and sort them out."

As the women settled into a comforting tea and pie routine, they momentarily set aside life's complexities and the tension seemed to melt away.

But all the while, Debbie was realizing that Wilma and Ada didn't fully support her decision to marry Fritz.

That led to a feeling of unease. She often looked to the two older women for advice.

CHAPTER 11

AFTER SHE FINISHED the pie and the hot tea, Debbie felt a need to escape from the scrutinizing gaze of Wilma and Ada. She needed fresh air and a moment to process her feelings, so she made her way to the barn.

The barn, with its familiar scent of hay and the low murmur of the animals, was always a place of comfort for Debbie. It reminded her of her childhood days, of simpler times when life's decisions weren't as weighted.

She reached for the telephone and dialed Fritz's number.

"Hello?"

"Fritz, it's me."

"Debbie! How are you? Is everything alright?" he asked.

"I'm okay," Debbie began, trying to choose her words carefully. "I just wanted to hear your voice. I miss you."

"Me too."

"Things are getting quite busy here, what with the wedding preparations and all."

There was a brief pause on the line before Fritz replied, "I can't wait to be there, Debbie. To start our new life together."

The sincerity in his voice made Debbie's heart flutter. "Have you been keeping busy?"

"I've had my hands full, but nothing's more important than us right now."

Debbie hesitated.

"How's Jared? Is he excited about the wedding?"

"Very much so." She debated telling Fritz about the recent incident but decided against it.

"I trust you to handle things there. I wish I could be with you now." There was a deep yearning in his voice, but before Debbie could reply, Fritz quickly added, "I should go. Things are a bit hectic here."

She frowned slightly. "Again? Fritz, is everything okay?"

"Everything's fine, but I'm so busy with organizing everything. Don't worry about me."

Before she could delve deeper, Fritz had already said his quick goodbye. The call ended, and Debbie was left feeling unsatisfied. She'd needed more. She needed him to say he loved her.

She leaned against a wooden beam, feeling the rough texture under her fingers. She trusted Fritz, but the hurried nature of their conversations lately made her wonder.

She knew preparing for their life together would be busy, but she couldn't help but feel there was something he wasn't telling her. With the wedding approaching, the weight of commitment and the fear of the unknown hung heavy in the air.

Debbie made her way back to the house, telling herself that she'd feel much better when Fritz arrived. He was moving here for good—moving here for her because he loved her.

CHAPTER 12

DEBBIE WOKE THE FOLLOWING MORNING, pleased she'd had a good night's sleep. After she got dressed, she gently nudged the door to Jared's room open.

"Time to get up, Jared. You don't want to be late for school," she said.

From beneath the covers came a feeble groan. "*Mamm*, I don't feel so good."

Debbie approached and sat on the edge of his bed, placing a comforting hand on his forehead. It felt hot. "What's wrong?"

Jared peeked from beneath his quilt, his eyes slightly glassy. "It's all those vegetables I've been eating," he mumbled, making Debbie chuckle.

She knew how much he loved school, and it was unlike him to want to skip it.

"You sure it's the vegetables and not that math test you mentioned last week?" she teased, knowing full well that wasn't the cause. Her concern deepened when he didn't respond with his usual playful defiance. "Do you think you're well enough to come with me to the markets? There's nowhere to lie down, but you can sit down."

"I think I just need to rest today. Can I stay home? I won't be any trouble."

Debbie brushed his dark hair away from his eyes. "Alright. I'll see if Wilma can watch over you today. Just try to get some sleep, okay?"

"Okay."

Debbie leaned down and kissed him lightly on his forehead.

Wilma was tidying up the kitchen when Debbie walked in, a furrow of concern etched on her forehead. The aroma of freshly baked bread wafted through the air, but Debbie barely noticed.

"Wilma, I've got to work today, but Jared isn't feeling well."

Wilma's hands stopped their motion of wiping down the counter, turning her full attention to Debbie. "What's wrong with him?"

Debbie shrugged her shoulders. "He's complaining of a sore tummy. I think he might've caught a bug or something. He's blaming the vegetables."

A glint of understanding flashed in Wilma's eyes. "Ah, yes, we were giving him extras after the joke he played, but I don't think they can make him ill."

Debbie nodded. "He is a little hotter than normal. I can't afford to miss today, especially with the wedding expenses coming up."

Wilma smiled warmly. "Don't you worry. I'll watch over Jared for you. You go on and tend to your tea stall. We'll manage just fine here."

Debbie smiled. "Thank you, Wilma. I was hoping you'd say that, but I didn't want to impose."

Wilma chuckled softly. "Impose? Nonsense! Jared is family. Besides, it'll allow me to spend time with him. I'll miss him when he's gone. Now, go on, get yourself ready. I'll check on Jared."

The two women walked toward Jared's room, where they found him curled up in bed, clutching his stomach.

"Good morning, Jared." Wilma sat down beside him.

Jared looked up, his face a shade paler than usual. "Hi."

Wilma felt his forehead with the back of her hand, assessing his temperature. "How are you feeling?"

"My tummy hurts," Jared mumbled, grimacing slightly. "I think I ate too many vegetables last night."

Wilma raised an eyebrow in amusement, sharing a knowing glance with Debbie. "Too many vegetables, you say? That's a first."

Jared pouted, looking genuinely miserable. "I promise, Aunt Wilma. I didn't sneak any cookies or candies. I couldn't find any."

Debbie stifled a chuckle, leaning down to kiss Jared's forehead. "You rest up, okay? Aunt Wilma will look after you. I'll bring home a treat for you."

Jared's eyes brightened momentarily at the prospect

of a treat, but then he groaned again, hugging his stomach.

Wilma winked at Debbie. "Go on now. We'll be fine."

As Debbie hurried off to prepare for her day, Wilma turned her attention back to Jared. "Now, let's see if we can't find something to help that tummy of yours. Maybe a warm compress, hmm?"

"I guess."

"Or maybe a dose of castor oil."

"No. It's too oily."

Wilma laughed. "It is oil."

"The warm thing would be better."

"Okay. We'll start with that. And maybe we'll give you a day off vegetables."

"Yes, please."

CHAPTER 13

AT MERCY'S home in the Amish community of Rivers Bend, she sighed, staring at her family's clothes scattered across her bed. A small mountain range of shirts, trousers, and socks lay before her, waiting to be neatly packed into their luggage. With two lively boys darting around the room, her head was spinning.

The younger, with his tousled blonde hair and wide-eyed innocence, handed Mercy a pair of socks. "Ma, do these go in too?" he asked, waving them like a whimsical flag.

"Thank you," Mercy responded, trying to hide her frustration with a smile.

The slightly older and more rebellious of the two took his shirt off and tossed it into the already-packed suitcase, a triumphant smirk lighting his face. "I helped!"

Mercy chuckled, her heart softening at the sight of their genuine efforts. "Yes, you did. Thank you." She folded the shirt neatly before placing it back into the suitcase.

From the doorway, a playful whistle pierced the chaotic melody of the packing. With his arms crossed in front of him, Stephen leaned against the frame, his dark eyes glinting with amusement. "Looks like a tornado swept through here," he mused, his voice carrying a light, teasing note.

Mercy shot him a less than amused glance. "Your tornado consists of two little cyclones, also known as our sons. Maybe you'd like to help rein them in?"

Stephen chuckled, sauntering into the room. Instead of lending a hand, he scooped up Timothy, spinning him around, much to the little boy's delight. "Do it again!" Timothy squealed.

But Mercy was not in the mood for games. Her eyebrows knitted together, forming a firm line above her eyes. "Stephen, this is not helping," she said, barely keeping her voice steady.

Stephen set the younger one down, allowing the boy to wobble off, dizzy but giggling.

"Hey, what's the matter?"

"Stephen," Mercy began, her voice almost a whisper, "I appreciate the joy and light-heartedness you bring into our home, especially with the fun and games when you come home. I work all the time and sometimes I need help."

He tilted his head slightly, the mischievous twinkle in his eyes softening into a more tender light. "I'm sorry, Mercy," he murmured, brushing a loose strand of hair from her forehead. "Sometimes I forget that there's a time for play and a time for work."

She sighed, leaning into his touch for a moment before pulling back. "I need you to fold the boys' clothes and pack them into the suitcase. The car's coming early tomorrow, and we need to be ready. Can you do that?"

Stephen nodded, his voice holding a gentle firmness. "Yes, Mercy. I can and I will."

He moved to the bed, picking up a small shirt and folding it meticulously, a soft smile playing on his lips as he glanced toward his wife. Mercy was a little irritated that he took nothing seriously.

The boys, sensing the shift in energy, circled back, their little hands reaching to help with the folding and packing.

As the room settled into a rhythm of cooperative packing, Mercy's thoughts wandered to Wilma's house. She couldn't wait to be back home, back at the apple orchard.

CHAPTER 14

A FEW MILES AWAY, Honor stood back, observing the neatly laid-out assortments of clothing on her bed. Everything was meticulously organized, as always. Their luggage stood open, waiting to be packed, but it seemed Jonathon, her husband, had everything well in hand as usual.

Jonathon turned from the dresser, holding neatly folded garments, his movements sure and efficient. "Honor, I've sorted the boys' clothing. Do you think they'll need extra jackets for the evenings?"

Honor smiled warmly, her heart swelling with affection for the man who always seemed to anticipate needs before she even voiced them. "That sounds wonderful, Jonathon. I think an extra jacket will be perfect, given how cold the weather's been."

In the room's corner, their two boys were playing a game of checkers.

"Boys, once you're done with your game, come and

choose what toy you'd like to bring," Honor called to them, her voice gentle yet carrying an edge of authority. "You can have one each, but no more. Make it small so you can bring it in the car with you."

Ephraim, the youngest, looked up, his blue eyes bright. "Can I bring my new horse, *Mamm?*"

"Of course," she replied.

The older brother carefully made his decision to pick a book while the younger one went to get his toy.

Jonathon, having overheard the exchange, gave Honor a sidelong glance, a playful smile tugging at the corners of his mouth. "They're growing up fast, aren't they?"

"They are," Honor agreed, a soft laugh escaping her. "And they're learning from the best." She gestured appreciatively at the nearly packed luggage.

Jonathon's smile widened as he resumed his task, tucking items into the suitcase with practiced ease. The room was peaceful, filled with a quiet, efficient energy that Honor knew was a direct reflection of Jonathon's unflappable nature. There was an undercurrent of excitement about the upcoming trip. Everyone was looking forward to it.

Finishing the last bit of packing, Jonathon closed the suitcases and lined them up near the door. "There we are. All set for Debbie's wedding," he announced, dusting off his hands.

Honor nodded, her heart full. "Thank you, Jonathon. I don't know how I got so blessed with you."

She wrapped her arms around him, her head resting against his chest.

"Well, I do," Jonathon quipped, his arms encircling her. "It's because you prayed really hard, and God had to get you off His back."

Honor laughed, swatting him playfully. "Oh, you!" She stepped back, a mock stern look on her face. "You should be glad I prayed that hard."

"Every day, I am," he replied sincerely, pulling her in for another hug.

CHAPTER 15

JARED STARTED FEELING MUCH BETTER and insisted he get a start on his daily chores. While Wilma was kneading the dough for bread, a familiar rhythmic clopping of hooves approached. She peered through the window and smiled, recognizing Eli's buggy pulling up the gravel driveway.

After she washed her hands and dried them, Wilma stepped outside, the door gently closing behind her. The breeze played with her hair, escaping from her *kapp,* as she hurriedly approached Eli, who was just getting down from his buggy.

"Eli," she greeted him with a bright smile. "I had a feeling today might be the day you'd drop by."

His eyes crinkled in amusement. "Always looking for ways to put me to work, aren't you?"

She laughed. "Not always. But today, I do have a special request."

"Alright, alright. What's on your mind, Wilma?"

She hesitated for a moment, glancing toward the stables where the faint sound of Jared's activities could be heard. Gathering her thoughts, she turned back to Eli. "It's about Jared. He said he was sick this morning, but he's better now, and he's insisting on doing his chores." She sighed, taking a moment and then she told him about the vegetable note incident. "Debbie and I have had a talk with him, but I believe he might heed the message better from someone he looks up to. Someone like you."

Eli's eyebrows knitted together, a mixture of surprise and curiosity. "Using a note for mischief, eh?"

"Yes, and Debbie hasn't been herself since that happened. I can tell she's worried that Jared will cause Fritz some strife after they're married. I can tell you from my experience it's not easy for a stepparent when their stepchildren misbehave. You're reluctant to scold them, and the resentment builds when they continue with their naughtiness."

"What would you like me to do, Wilma?"

"We want him to understand the implications of his actions, not just the immediate laughter or shock value they might bring. Sometimes, a different voice, especially one with the wisdom of years, might drive the point home."

A slow nod came from Eli. "I remember the antics of my youth and the lessons they brought with them. Alright, Wilma, I'll have a chat with the boy. It might do him some good to hear a tale or two from my days."

Gratitude shone in Wilma's eyes. "Thank you, Eli. I knew you'd be able to help."

"Not a problem, Wilma," Eli assured her, tipping his hat slightly. "Now, let me go find that young rascal."

"He's in there." She nodded toward the barn. "And when you're through, I'll have a cup of coffee and a piece of cake waiting for you."

"I'll look forward to that." Eli, wearing his work clothes, well-worn hat, and sturdy boots, approached the stables while Wilma hurried back to the house.

The muffled sound of hay being shuffled and the occasional grunt indicated Jared was hard at work inside.

Pushing open the barn door, Eli was greeted by the sight of the small boy, pitchfork in hand, focused on mucking out a stall. The scent of hay, horse, and leather mixed in the air.

"Hello, Jared."

Jared looked up in surprise. "Hi, Eli."

"Aren't you supposed to be sick?" Eli asked him.

"I'm feeling better. I'll only have to do this later. It's one of my chores."

"Good idea. You're doing it now, so you don't have to do it later?"

"Yeah. Have you come to help me?"

"I thought maybe we could share some stories," Eli replied with a twinkle in his eye. "But first, I heard about your little note prank. Quite the trickster, huh?"

Jared leaned the pitchfork against the wall. "I guess I didn't think it through. They'll always watch me now to make sure that I eat the vegetables. I can't give them to Red like I used to. I think I must be allergic to veggies or something."

Eli chuckled. "You used to give your veggies to Red?"

"Yeah. Red will eat anything."

Eli leaned against a stable beam, his gaze steady on Jared. "You know, when I was your age, I played my fair share of pranks. Some turned out to be harmless fun, while others... well, let's just say they didn't end up well."

Jared looked up, curiosity piqued. "Really? Like, what pranks did you do?"

Eli chuckled, "Well, there was this one time I thought it'd be funny to switch out the sugar for salt. Imagine the look on my ma's face when she took a sip of her morning coffee. She got two spoonfuls of salt instead of sugar." Eli laughed at the memory, but then his expression turned serious. "But the real issue came when she used that salt to bake pies for a community gathering. Those pies were inedible, and my ma was horrified. Word got around that she was a dreadful baker."

Jared smiled. "That's a good one. Swap the sugar and the salt."

"It was," Eli nodded, "but it taught me a valuable lesson about consequences. Everything we do has a consequence. Even the little things. Fun is fun, but not at the expense of others."

Jared grinned. "Aunt Wilma already gave me a talk, but you make more sense."

Eli took a step toward Jared. "Good to hear. Remember, it's all about balance. A joke here and there is fine, but always think about how it might affect others. And if you're ever in doubt, maybe it's a sign to think twice."

Jared nodded, absorbing Eli's words. "Thanks, Eli. I'll remember that."

Eli sat down on a hay bale, crossing his arms. "You know, Jared, it's one thing to realize when you've done something that wasn't quite right. But the proper measure of a man's character is what he does after. Can you think of a way to make amends for the pranks you pulled? Or even just a good deed to spread some joy?"

Jared's brow furrowed in thought, his fingers drumming rhythmically against his chin. The stable was filled with the warm, muted sounds of animals shifting and the distant hum of insects. After a few moments, his eyes lit up with inspiration. "I remember when we built that birdhouse. Every time I see birds using it, it makes me happy. What if I build more birdhouses for people? Is that what you mean?"

Eli grinned. "Make more birdhouses?"

"*Jah*, lots of them."

"That's a wonderful idea, Jared. Not only would it provide something for the birds, but it would also bring joy to many in the community. It's a way of giving back, creating something positive out of your realization."

Jared's eyes glowed with enthusiasm, but a hint of uncertainty remained. "Would you... um, would you be able to help me like you did with the first one? The one we made turned out so great because of you. Aunt Wilma wasn't doing such a good job and then you fixed it."

Eli nodded. "Of course. I'd be honored to help you. And I believe it'll be a step in the right direction for you. By creating something of value, you're choosing a path of kindness and generosity. That's the mark of true growth."

"Thank you, Eli. I can't wait to get started."

"I noticed last time that there's plenty of spare wood in the workshop we can use. What plans do you have for today?" Eli asked.

"Nothing."

"Why don't we make a start right now?"

"For real?" Jared asked.

"Yes, when you finish your chores. I've got a cup of coffee waiting for me, so I'll be back out in fifteen minutes and we can start then."

As Eli made his way back to the house, the warm, comforting aroma of freshly baked bread and brewing coffee welcomed him. Inside, Wilma had set a place for him at the kitchen table, a generous slice of cake accompanying the steaming mug.

"How did your talk with Jared go?" Wilma asked.

Settling into the chair, Eli took a sip of his coffee before responding. "Better than expected. That boy is a whirlwind of energy and ideas, but he's got a good heart." He savored a bite of cake, appreciating the familiar comfort in its sweetness. "We had a long talk about actions and consequences. And you know, I think he understood. He's just trying to find his way, testing boundaries like all young ones do."

Wilma listened, her expression softening. "That's reassuring to hear. I often worry I might be too hard on the boy, expecting too much."

Eli shook his head, offering a reassuring smile. "You're doing just fine. Jared respects you; that much is clear. But sometimes, it helps to hear things from a different person. Today, we also found something where he can focus all his energy."

Intrigued, Wilma leaned in slightly. "Oh? What might that be?"

"He's planning to build birdhouses and wants to make a lot of them. He figured it would bring joy to others, and well, it's his way of making amends," Eli explained.

A smile bloomed across Wilma's face. "That's wonderful. It sounds just like something he would come up with. Creative, yet thoughtful. I'm glad he has you to guide him, Eli."

Eli took a mouthful of coffee. "It gives me something to do."

Just as Eli had finished his refreshments, Ada arrived, and Eli went to the barn to find Jared.

Over the next few hours, the workshop was filled with the sounds of sawing, hammering, and laughter. Eli patiently guided Jared through each step, reminding him of the importance of precision and care. They recalled the memories of making the first birdhouse, their mistakes, and the lessons they'd learned.

Jared's face beamed with pride as a new, much larger birdhouse took shape.

Finally, as the afternoon sun moved, leaving the workshop darker, they moved onto the porch to finish it.

Ada came out of the front door and stared at them. "What's with all the noise?"

"Look, Ada. It's a birdhouse for someone special to make them happy."

Ada raised her eyebrows. "That's so thoughtful of you. Make sure you clean up your mess, Jared."

"I'll see that it's all cleared, Ada," Eli said.

"No, Eli, let Jared do the cleanup. He needs to learn responsibility."

"Sure. I'll leave that for him."

Ada moved back inside and closed the door behind her.

Finally, the new birdhouse was complete. It was an unpainted replica of the first.

Jared's face was a mix of pride and satisfaction. "It's perfect, Eli. Thank you. I might paint it a different color."

"Hmm. Not too bright. You don't want to scare the birds away." Eli, wiping the sweat from his brow, smiled at Jared. "Remember, homes change, and surroundings change, but memories always remain. This birdhouse is a testament to that."

Jared looked up at him. "What do you mean?"

"We'll have this memory for a long time. When you get older, memories will become important. I hope when I've gone home to Gott that you'll take a moment to think about today."

"I don't want you to go anywhere." Jared flung his arms around Eli, the birdhouse cradled in his arms.

"I'll be around for a while, Gott willing."

Jared looked down at the birdhouse. "I love this birdhouse. Thank you for helping me. Who will I give it to?"

"Any person you want. Your mother's wedding's coming up. How about you give it to her?" He gave Jared a wink.

Jared tried to wink back, but he ended up winking with both eyes. "Yeah, it can be our secret."

"I'll leave you to clean up out here. I'll see if Wilma and Ada can make this old man another cup of coffee, and maybe there will be some cake left." He ruffled Jared's hair before he went inside the house.

CHAPTER 16

ADA ARRIVED at Wilma's house the next morning not feeling too good. With Wilma in the kitchen, Ada moved to the porch. With no one around, she peeled off her stockings and stretched out her legs, reveling in the sensation of sunlight warming her pale skin.

"It always makes me feel better," she murmured to herself, closing her eyes and tilting her head back, "especially on days when I don't feel my best."

After some time, Ada decided she needed a glass of water. When she placed her foot down, she felt a sharp, searing pain. She let out a sharp cry, hopping on one foot and reaching down to see what had caused the agony. To her dismay, she found a nail embedded in the sole of her foot.

Remembering the recent activities around the house, Ada's face turned a shade redder. "Jared!" she exclaimed, more out of pain than anger.

Knowing she needed immediate attention, Ada

called out for help, hoping someone would come to her aid soon. Jared's careless actions had clear repercussions, and he was about to learn the importance of being responsible.

Wilma heard her yells and rushed to her side.

"Jared was working on those birdhouses right here on the porch! I told him to be careful!"

Taking in the situation with a quick glance, Wilma immediately helped Ada inside and then grabbed a basin of warm water and some clean cloths.

Carefully, Wilma removed the nail and cleaned the wound meticulously with iodine before wrapping it in a bandage.

With Ada resting comfortably and her foot elevated, Wilma couldn't help but shake her head in disbelief. "I thought Jared had learned his lesson," she sighed. "But no. He's not even responsible for cleaning up after himself."

"I know. It probably wasn't a good idea for them to work on the porch. What shall we do about it? Perhaps we shouldn't be too mad at him. He takes things so personally."

"This *is* personal because it's about him, Wilma. First, the vegetable note from me, supposedly, and now his carelessness has caused me a lot of pain."

Wilma, her eyes clouded with worry, cradled Ada's bandaged foot. "I can't believe this happened. It was unfortunate, but it was an accident."

"Tell that to my foot!" Ada winced, both from the pain and the topic at hand. "I know he's young and prone to a bit of mischief, but this isn't just mischief. This was neglectful."

Nodding in agreement, Wilma sighed deeply. "I suppose he has to understand that his actions have repercussions, not just for him, but for everyone around him."

Gritting her teeth, Ada added, "And it's not just about picking up after himself. It's about safety, consideration, and responsibility."

Wilma took a moment, gathering her thoughts. "Eli had a talk with him and—"

"He needs a proper talking-to. Eli is too gentle. Maybe he needs some added responsibilities around the house so he can grasp the importance of being meticulous." Ada smirked despite her discomfort. "A few more chores might just do the trick."

Wilma chuckled softly. "Or at least keep him occupied enough to stay out of trouble. It's up to Debbie to punish him though. It's not our place."

"True." Ada gave a nod. "But perhaps if Debbie had been more strict with him, then I wouldn't be in so much pain right now."

Wilma bit her lip. She didn't like these unpleasant situations. For Debbie's sake, she had to intervene. "I'll have a word to him before Debbie gets home. I don't want her to get upset right before the wedding."

"Good idea, Wilma." Ada's mouth turned down at the corners.

CHAPTER 17

BEFORE JARED COULD EVEN DROP his bag when he came home, Wilma gestured to his room. "Go to your room, Jared."

"What did I do?" Wilma pointed to Ada's bandaged foot. "You left a nail on the porch. It ended up deeply into Ada's foot."

His mouth fell open. "I thought I got all the nails."

Ada frowned at him. "Is that all you can say? Maybe there is another word starting with S?"

"Sorry, Ada."

"Hmm. We'll discuss this later."

Jared ran up the stairs and ran into his room. Wilma felt bad and took him some milk and cookies.

As soon as Wilma entered his room, he blurted out, "I didn't mean to do it, Aunt Wilma."

"I know you didn't."

"How long am I going to be in my room?"

Wilma felt caught in the middle. She couldn't let him out of the room right now because Ada would think she didn't care about her injured foot or didn't care about raising Jared to be more careful. "Not long. Just until your mother comes home."

"Okay."

Wilma sat on the edge of his bed. "We don't want to upset your mother before the wedding, do we?"

"No."

"I know it was an accident. It's just unfortunate that you wrote that note pretending it was from Ada, and now the nail ended up in her foot."

"Sorry."

"Just take some time to think about how you can avoid both those things from happening in the future. Okay?"

"Yes, Aunt Wilma." Jared reached for a cookie and bit into it while Wilma quietly closed his door.

Several minutes later, Debbie arrived home to find Wilma in the kitchen, her face etched with worry. "What's happened now?" she inquired, sensing something was amiss.

With a sigh, Wilma recounted the events of the day. Debbie's face darkened with each detail, her concern evident. Heading to Jared's room, she knocked softly before entering. She found Jared sitting on his bed, his face a picture of guilt.

"Jared," Debbie began, trying to keep her voice calm, "do you understand what you've done?"

Jared nodded, his eyes shiny with unshed tears. "I'm

really sorry, *Mamm.* I know I should've been more careful. I just... I didn't think I left any nails. Maybe someone else did it."

"That's unlikely." Debbie sighed, taking a moment to collect her thoughts. "This isn't just about being careful, Jared. It's about understanding the consequences of your actions even if it was an accident."

Jared lowered his head, his voice a whisper. "I'm sorry. I said sorry to Ada."

Taking a deep breath, Debbie said, "I want you to apologize to Ada again. But remember, actions speak louder than words. You need to make things right."

Jared nodded. He took his mother's hand, and they both walked down the steps. Jared found Ada in the kitchen.

"I'm really sorry, Ada. I won't do it again."

Ada smiled weakly, patting the chair beside her. "Come here," she whispered. "I know it was an accident, right?"

"Yeah."

"You didn't mean any harm. Let this be a lesson."

"I hate these lessons," Jared yelled out.

Ada moved back, shocked by his outburst. "I think you need to go to your room and think about your manners."

Jared turned and ran away.

"Where's he going?" Ada asked.

Wilma listened for a moment. "I can hear him running up to his room."

Debbie stood there frozen, unsure of what to do.

More importantly, how would Fritz handle Jared's outbursts?

CHAPTER 18

Jared was upset about being blamed for what was nothing but an accident. He didn't deserve to be put in his room.

Inspired by Eli's stories of mischief from his childhood, he thought about swapping the salt and the sugar around when no one was looking. Then he recalled how high the salt was kept in the pantry.

He decided to stick with an idea that had already worked for him—notes.

He had to get to Matthew. He had another great idea for Ada. She'd been so mean.

He looked out his window, wondering how to get away from the house with no one seeing. It didn't help that his window was so high off the ground.

There was a tree close by. Perhaps he could jump to it, but if he fell… it was a long way to the bottom. Instead, with his pencil case and notepad, he creeped out of his bedroom and tiptoed to the top of the stairs.

Hearing all the voices coming from the kitchen, he knew no one was in the living room.

He ambled down the steps and once he was at the bottom, he sprinted to the front door. Then he ran away as fast as he could through the orchard, searching for Matthew.

He found him carefully inspecting some of the younger saplings. "Matthew," Jared called out.

Matthew looked up, his face breaking into a smile. "What can I do for you today?"

"I want more practice writing. Can you jot down a few notes for me so I can copy them?" Jared asked.

Matthew chuckled, raising an eyebrow, "Alright, but these better not be for another prank. I heard you used my vegetable note and got yourself into a spot of strife."

"Yeah. I got in so much trouble and now they give me more vegetables, enough to make me sick."

Matthew laughed again. "Backfired, did it?"

"I guess so." Handing over a pen and paper, Jared dictated a few lines, grinning mischievously as Matthew scribbled them down.

"I hope no one ever sees these," Matthew remarked, glancing over the words.

"They won't," Jared assured him, tucking the notes safely into his pencil case. "Thanks, Matthew!"

"Anytime, young friend." Matthew chuckled.

Feeling emboldened, Jared was ready to head back to the house. He'd achieved his mission, but getting back unseen would be the real challenge.

He made his way toward the rear entrance of the home, using the tall hedges and garden structures as cover. Approaching the back door, he took a moment to peer through the window, ensuring no one was around.

Seeing the coast was clear, he quietly slipped inside and tiptoed up the staircase. Every creak of the wooden steps had him holding his breath. As he reached the top, familiar voices from the kitchen reached his ears, signaling that everyone was still engrossed in their chatter.

Taking the opportunity, he quickly darted across the hallway and slipped back into his room, his heart pounding.

Safely in his bedroom, he took the note out and hid it under his pillow for another day.

CHAPTER 19

RUTH'S CAR hummed smoothly along the country roads on the way to the Baker Apple Orchard. Cherish and Favor sat in the back, side by side, with the vast expanse of the car seat between them, and Harriet sat in the front.

Ruth kept glancing in her rearview mirror. "I'm looking forward to this. I haven't even been away from home in ages."

Harriet, however, looked less than pleased. She stared out the window, her nose upturned as though she smelled something foul. Every bump or sudden brake made her cluck her tongue in disapproval. "The suspension in this car isn't too good," she finally said. "It's better in a buggy."

"It's the roads," Ruth explained. "This car is more for city driving. That's why I also have my truck. It's better suited to the country, but it's no good for long drives." Ruth glanced at Harriet. "Don't worry, the roads will get better soon."

Cherish, sensing the mounting tension, tried to change the subject. "It's been so long since we've seen Debbie. I can't believe she's finally getting married and Jared will finally have a father."

Favor nodded, but her face turned a shade greener. "Can we... umm... stop for a moment?" she whispered, her hand clutching her belly.

Ruth quickly pulled over and stopped. Favor staggered out, leaning over to catch her breath.

Harriet rushed over with a bottle of water. "Should we turn back? Will you be okay?"

Favor took the bottle from her and took a mouthful. "I'll be fine. I can't miss this."

"I think maybe we should turn back. Then Cherish and Ruth can continue on their own."

"No, it's fine. I just need to get fresh air for a moment." Favor started walking around.

Ruth took the time to get out of the car and stretch her arms over her head.

Once Favor felt better, they resumed their journey, the car now filled with the soft hum of a radio playing country tunes.

Time seemed to stretch on, but finally, the familiar sight of the apple orchard came into view.

Ruth parked the car near the entrance, and the group got out of the car.

A wave of relief washed over Favor as she stepped

onto the familiar ground. "Thank you for driving us, Ruth."

Ruth smiled. "Anytime, dear."

Cherish and Favor looked at the vast orchard before them, their hearts filled with nostalgia as childhood memories came rushing back.

As they headed toward their childhood house, Favor whispered to Cherish, "I just hope Harriet behaves herself."

Cherish chuckled. "It's going to be an eventful few days. I can feel it."

Mamm was the first to rush out and greet them, her eyes sparkling with joy. She made a beeline for her daughters, wrapping her arms around them.

Then she put her hand over Favor's tummy and started talking to the unborn child.

Cherish laughed. "Breathe, *Mamm*, breathe."

"I'm breathing. This is the first time I've seen Favor pregnant. I can't wait to be a grandmother to this little one."

"You'll have a few months to wait, *Mamm*." Favor laughed.

"Come and get warm in the house."

Cherish got the suitcases out of the trunk, and Harriet helped. Once they'd done that, they headed to the house.

After ensuring Favor was comfortably seated, Harriet approached Ada.

"It's been too long," Ada remarked, reaching out to grasp Harriet's hand.

"Some things never change," Harriet replied, her eyes flitting toward Favor protectively.

Cherish stared at Ada's bandaged foot. "What happened to you, Ada?"

"Oh, I'll tell you all about it another time. How was your trip?"

"It was a journey, to say the least," Favor replied, recalling her bouts of nausea during the drive. "I'm just glad all the movement has stopped. Although, I still feel like I'm moving."

Cherish nodded, adding, "It was an interesting drive with Harriet's running commentary on Ruth's driving."

Ada raised an eyebrow. "Oh, Harriet, were you giving Ruth a hard time?"

Harriet, looking slightly affronted, responded, "I was just pointing out the bumps in the road, ensuring we didn't miss any."

Ruth, with a laugh, waved it off. "All in a day's work. Honestly, I'm just glad we're here."

"Well, get ready for an experience. Debbie's wedding is set to be the talk of the community," Cherish said.

Favor looked again at Ada's bandaged foot. "Do tell us what happened to you, Ada?"

Ada sighed dramatically, "Ah, a minor accident involving a nail and Jared's birdhouse project."

Harriet clicked her tongue. "That's disappointing and careless."

Mamm chimed in, "He certainly keeps us on our toes." Wilma then turned to Ruth. "Thank you for driving them. It means a lot. It would've been much more pleasant than going in a hired car."

Ruth shrugged, smiling. "It's just a drive. Besides, it's beautiful here. When I'm not so tired, I'd like to have a look around the orchard."

"I'll give you a tour when you feel up to it. Where are you staying?" Wilma asked.

"I've booked a bed-and-breakfast."

"Oh, you didn't have to do that. We could've found someone for you to stay with, or we could've squeezed you in here."

Ruth shook her head. "No. It's fine. I don't want to put anyone out."

"You'll be staying at my house, Harriet," Ada said.

"I'd love that. I wasn't sure where I'd stay. It was all so last minute. I told Favor if she was coming, then I'd come too to make sure she doesn't overdo things."

CHAPTER 20

"Ruth!" Jed saw her as soon as he pulled the buggy up. He jumped out and ran to her, embracing her in a warm hug that spoke volumes of their bond.

Ruth laughed as she stepped back. "Look at you, all grown-up and responsible."

"I can't believe you're here. It means a lot that you came."

Ruth gave him a tender, motherly look. "I wouldn't have missed it for the world. I had to see how my boy was doing, after all. So, tell me everything. How have you been?" Ruth inquired, her gaze soft yet inquisitive.

"Let's sit for a moment." They sat on the porch and then he continued. "I'm staying here, Ruth. This community, it's become home. And there's more," he hesitated for a fraction of a second before continuing, "Krystal and I, we're serious. I plan to marry her."

Ruth's hand flew to her heart, her eyes misting with emotion. "Oh, Jed, that's wonderful news. I guessed it. I saw how you both got along. It was instant. Love at first sight?"

"I guess it was," Jed chuckled, unable to hide his excitement. "I've started a touring business. It's seasonal, but it's something I'm passionate about. And Krystal, she's doing amazing with her quilt store. We believe we'll make a good living between the two of us."

"I always knew you'd find your path, Jed. I'm so proud of you. But I'll admit, the house does feel empty without you. It's a little upsetting when I walk past the room off from the barn where you used to stay."

"I miss you too, Ruth. How's the farm doing?"

"All is well. The animals are keeping me busy, and the land has been generous this year."

"That's good to hear. Promise to come back for our wedding, though? I can't imagine that day without you."

Ruth laughed lightly. "I promise, though you're keeping me in suspense here without a date."

"We haven't set one yet, but you'll be the first to know," Jed assured her.

"I should go inside and talk with everyone. I mainly came to check up on you," she confessed with a twinkle in her eye.

Jed hugged her again, tighter this time. "I'm glad you did."

"Are you coming inside?"

"I am."

CHAPTER 21

LATER, when Ruth left to check in at the bed-and-breakfast, everyone moved to the kitchen.

Cherish's gaze landed on a furry, reddish-brown dog sprawled comfortably on a rug. "Who's this?" she asked.

Wilma smiled affectionately at the dog. "That's Red."

Ada was last into the kitchen. "Quite a story behind that one."

Cherish crouched down, extending her hand for the dog to sniff. Red wagged his tail, pressing his nose into her palm. "Red? That's an interesting name."

Ada chuckled. "It's not just the name that's interesting. Wilma found him as a stray, you know."

Cherish blinked in surprise, looking up at her mother. "You brought home a stray? Since when do you bring animals, especially strays, and allow them into the house? You hate animals. I can't believe this.

97

You were always trying to get Caramel out of the house."

Wilma sighed, a soft smile touching her lips. "Red came to me. I didn't bring him home. He just appeared."

Ada added, "The poor thing was being cruelly treated. Your mother couldn't stand by and watch. She took him off his owner and rescued him."

Cherish looked from Ada to Wilma, her eyes wide. *"Mamm,* I never thought I'd see the day you'd let a dog into the house, let alone rescue one."

Wilma reached down to scratch Red behind the ears. "Neither did I. But there's something about Red. He's special."

Red let out a contented sigh, snuggling closer to Wilma's feet.

"Well, I can see he's already made himself quite at home. I guess miracles happen. I never thought I'd see anything like this. It's so out of the ordinary for you, *Mamm."*

"Well, things have changed. You should be pleased." Wilma gave a nod.

Cherish patted the dog some more. "Welcome to the family, Red."

The room was filled with chatter and laughter when Debbie entered the house, Jared in tow. The moment the door opened, a noticeable shift in energy occurred. Heads turned and conversations paused as eyes fell on the bride-to-be.

"Debbie!" Cherish exclaimed, leaping from her seat

and wrapping her arms around her.

Favor, holding her slightly swollen belly, rose with a little more effort but was equally eager to greet Debbie. "It's been too long."

"Thanks for coming here. I'm so excited to see you both, and you too, Harriet."

Harriet, maintaining her usual reserved demeanor, simply nodded and offered a small smile. "You look well, dear."

Debbie returned each greeting with a warmth that lit up the room. "It's so wonderful to see all of you. I can't believe the wedding is just days away."

As the initial greetings waned, Jared, who had momentarily been overshadowed by the excitement surrounding his mother, found himself the center of attention. Cherish crouched down to his level. "Look how tall you've become, Jared."

He blushed but stood a little taller, clearly enjoying the attention. *"Mamm* says I'm growing like a weed."

Ada, her foot elevated but still very much involved in the gathering, chuckled. "That's right and just as hard to manage as a weed sometimes." She shot a teasing glance at Debbie, referring to the nail incident.

Debbie looked at all her friends. "I'm so happy to see you all."

"Speaking of cheerful things, let's see the dress," Favor said.

"I don't have it yet. Florence is making finishing touches to it."

"When can we see Florence?" Cherish squawked. "I can't wait to see the new baby."

"We can see her soon, maybe tomorrow," Debbie said.

Favor moved to the sink to get a glass of water. She looked up and saw a tall stranger. "Who's that out there?"

Wilma moved to stand beside her. "That's Gabe."

"Hey, Cherish. Gabe's Malachi's brother, isn't he?" Favor asked.

Cherish raced to the window. "Oh yes. He looks like Jed and Malachi." Cherish headed outside to meet him.

CHAPTER 22

CHERISH HAD HEARD whispers and snippets about Gabe, the elusive brother who had taken on temporary employment in the orchard.

Malachi had shared tales of a tumultuous upbringing, painting a picture of a family with its fair share of challenges. Cherish was eager to hear more about her husband's history.

Coming closer to Gabe, Cherish took a deep breath. His deep-set eyes were contemplative, as though lost in thought.

"Hi, you must be Gabe," she began. "I'm Cherish. Malachi's wife."

Gabe straightened up, offering a polite smile. "Ah, Cherish, it's a pleasure to finally meet. I've heard a lot about you."

She chuckled. "I've heard quite a bit about you too. Not all of it directly, though. You know, whispers here, stories there."

He raised an eyebrow, a hint of amusement in his eyes. "Stories, you say? I hope they weren't too exaggerated."

"Oh, just tales of adventures and a bit about growing up," she replied. "So, you're working here for a while?"

"Yeah, until the work runs out."

"I'm sorry to come straight to the point like this with us only just meeting and everything. Malachi has kept me away from his family, so it makes me wonder sometimes. Can you tell me a bit about your family, like your childhood?"

Gabe looked thoughtful for a moment. "Our childhood was... challenging, to say the least. Our parents' on-again, off-again relationship with the community, their personal struggles... it made for an unusual upbringing."

Cherish nodded. "Malachi mentioned some of it. It must have been hard for all of you."

Gabe sighed. "It was. But it also shaped us, made us who we are today. Challenges build character, or so they say. I hope it made us all stronger."

They continued to converse, with Cherish learning a little more about the brothers' shared history.

After several minutes, Cherish felt a deeper connection to her husband's family. She'd learned more from Gabe in a few minutes than she'd learned from her husband in all the years she'd been married to him.

Wilma interrupted them. "Gabe, would you have a meal with us tonight? You can meet Favor too."

He looked over at Wilma. "I'd love to. Thank you, Wilma. I'm eager to get to know everyone better."

"Good. We'll all appreciate your company," Wilma replied. "We're having a roast."

"That sounds great. I'll get cleaned up and I'll come back this evening."

Wilma and Cherish headed back to the house just as Samuel arrived.

Then Wilma set to work in the kitchen, her hands moving deftly as she seasoned the meat and prepared the vegetables. Soon, the comforting aroma of the roast filled the air, mingling with the sweet scent of the apple pie that would be their dessert.

"Wilma, that smells delicious. Sorry I can't help. I can't stand on my foot for too long." Ada said.

"That's fine. I thought I'd make something special since Gabe is coming over for dinner," Wilma said.

"Ah, Gabe," Ada remarked with a slight movement of her foot. "He's such a fine man."

Samuel nodded in agreement. "He certainly works hard."

LATER THAT EVENING, Krystal and Jed arrived followed by Gabe.

As they all gathered around the table, Wilma felt a contentment that had been missing lately.

Everyone bowed their heads in silent prayer before eating. When all eyes were opened, everyone started helping themselves to the food in the center of the table.

"Wilma," Debbie exclaimed in between bites, her cheeks pink with delight, "this roast is marvelous! You must share with me what herbs you used."

"Of course I will," Wilma replied.

"Wilma, I have to say, this is one of the best meals I've had in a long time," Gabe added, his gaze sincere. "Thank you for inviting me."

"You're welcome, Gabe. We're glad to have you here," Wilma responded.

As everyone shared stories and laughter, Debbie felt grateful for the people in her life.

Gabe's presence had brought an unexpected brightness to the evening.

Debbie watched as the brothers, Jed and Gabe, exchanged glances.

She could tell that Ada's curiosity was piqued as she leaned forward, her eyes twinkling with interest. "Jed, Gabe," Ada began, "I've been wondering about your family. Malachi has shared little about his kin, and neither have you, Jed. What can you tell us about your family?"

Gabe swallowed his mouthful, his eyes meeting Ada's. "Well, there are six of us sons. Our parents had some trouble in their early days. At one stage, all of us kids were split up, and we were living with different community members, but then everything came right."

"My, that must have been quite a lively household," Harriet commented.

"It was never dull," Jed chimed in, his dark eyes sparkling with memories. "There was always someone to play with or talk to."

"Speaking of Malachi," Cherish piped up. "Why is he so secretive? Anyone got any ideas?"

"Malachi is... complicated," Gabe explained, his expression somber. "He carries the weight of our father's expectations on his shoulders, and it's been difficult for him at times."

"Your father passed away last year, didn't he?" Ada asked gently, her empathy shining through.

Gabe shook his head. "No. He's still alive."

"Oh, I'm sorry." Ada looked down. "I must be thinking about someone else."

"May his soul rest in peace," Samuel murmured.

Ada frowned at Samuel. "Who?"

Samuel looked up. "The person you mistook for Gabe's father."

"Oh." Ada pursed her lips and looked away.

Debbie glanced at Jared as he sat by himself at the children's table. It can't have been easy being the only child in a single-parent family. She was so pleased that all that was going to change.

The conversation at the table then switched to Honor, Mercy, and their families, who were arriving the next day.

CHAPTER 23

THE FOLLOWING DAY, Ada and Harriet got to Wilma's house early so she wouldn't miss the arrival of Mercy and Honor.

They sat with Wilma on the porch, sharing a knitted blanket over their knees. Ada's bandaged foot was awkwardly propped up on a chair in front of her.

In front of the ladies, Red lay in a relaxed sprawl. His half-lidded eyes lazily tracked their conversation, seeming to relish the soothing tones of their voices.

Wilma sipped her hot tea, letting its warmth linger. "Once Debbie and Jared leave, and eventually Krystal marries Jed, this house... it's going to echo with silence. I'll wander through this house, listening to my own footsteps for company."

Ada glanced over at her. "Oh, come now, Wilma. You act as if solitude is your only future. Didn't you have a certain man showing interest just a while back?

But you let him just walk right out of your life." Ada shook her head. "I don't know why."

Wilma grinned, recalling the moments she had shared with Eli's cousin. "It was nice to think about, but I need to live in reality. I'm too old to live through losing another husband."

With a mischievous glint in her eyes, Ada teased, "Who knows? He might surprise you at Debbie's wedding. Imagine the scandal and the whispers."

"I'd like to meet him," Harriet said.

Wilma giggled. "There would be no scandal and I don't expect that he'll show. Sorry, Harriet, but I think he's gone for good."

"Speaking of companionship, there's always Eli."

Wilma sighed at Ada's playful torment. "Eli is a cherished friend, Ada, not someone I'd ever marry."

Ada leaned in closer. "You know, he speaks so fondly of his late wife. Annoying as that might be, it does show he's the kind of man who would be truly devoted."

Wilma laughed louder this time, making Red perk up. "You never stop, do you? Always seeing the world through your matchmaking eyes."

"Well, the best marriages are built on the foundation of friendship."

"Wilma, you should do what I did. If your child moves, you move with them. Then you won't be lonely." Harriet gave a nod.

"But I have six daughters and three stepchildren. Four of my daughters have moved away and one of my stepsons moved. I'd have to split myself up to do that. Besides that, I'm very much attached to this place."

Their conversation continued, filled with light-hearted banter and shared memories. All the while, Red shifted occasionally, trying to soak up the winter sun's rays.

Two black cars coming up the driveway interrupted them minutes later.

"Is this them, Wilma?" Harriet asked.

Wilma bounded to their feet. "It is. Oh, Ada, I don't know what to say to them about staying at your house." Wilma started heading to the door.

"Whooaa. Where are you going, Wilma?"

"To the kitchen before they see me. You come and get me after you've broken the news."

"But aren't you eager to see them?" Harriet asked.

"I am. I'll see them after you deliver the news. It will be better coming from you."

Ada's mouth fell open. She never figured she'd have to be the one to face Wilma's two eldest daughters to deliver the news that they were staying with her instead of their mother.

Ada huffed. "If only Wilma gave me some kind of warning to prepare myself. Honor will be okay with whatever preparations have been made, but Mercy will be furious."

Harriet stood. "Maybe I'll help Wilma in the kitchen. They've had a long drive, so I'll help with the refreshments." Harriet scurried into the house.

Left alone, Ada folded the blanket, placing it on the

chair beside her while she rehearsed a nice way to break the news. Then she took a big breath and faced the cars, wobbling on her sore foot.

Mercy was first out of the car, and when she was getting the boys out, she felt a hand on her shoulder. She turned around to see that it was Ada.

"Hi." Mercy wrapped her arms around Ada. "Where's *Mamm?*"

"Inside, but I must tell you that you and Honor and your families will be staying at my *haus.* There are already too many people staying here."

Mercy's heart sank as the boys scurried off. She wanted to be with her mother. She missed living at home and she'd been looking forward to this for months.

She huffed and looked over at the house while Ada greeted Honor and the others.

Another reason she wanted to stay at her mother's house was that she needed to talk with her mother in private. If she had to stay with Ada, when would she get a chance to talk privately with *Mamm?*

Mercy's eyes burned. She swallowed in an effort to stop the tears from coming. "I don't want to stay with you," Mercy said, turning away from Ada.

"You don't want to stay with me?" Ada's voice rose as if she was ready to argue with Mercy.

Mercy looked over at the boys running into the barn and turned back to Ada. "I want to stay with my mother. Why does this always happen every time I come here?"

Ada's eyes widened, caught off guard by Mercy's statement.

Honor hurried back over and stood next to Ada. "So we're staying with you?"

"Yes. It's all arranged." Ada nodded.

"It can be un-arranged." Mercy folded her arms and pouted.

"It'll be fine staying with Ada. The boys will all be together and they'll love that," Honor said.

"I wanna stay with *Mamm.*"

Ada shook her head. "You can't stay with her."

"Why not?" Mercy asked.

CHAPTER 24

"Why can't I stay here?" Mercy repeated.

"Because the house is full already, Mercy." Ada huffed.

Mercy put her hands on her hips. "Who is it full with?"

"You've got the boys, and your mother needs a quiet home as she gets the house ready for the wedding," Ada whispered.

Mercy felt her heart stop beating for a moment as she struggled to catch her breath. She tried to steady herself by moving forward and placing a hand on the porch railing. "Honor and Jonathon can stay with you. I'll talk with *Mamm* myself. Look, I've had a terrible time getting here. One boy was carsick, and we had to keep stopping. It was tortuous. The whole time, I kept thinking I'll be there soon, and I was thinking of staying here, in my old home." Mercy rushed past Ada and headed into the house.

"Hasn't changed one bit," Ada muttered under her breath.

Mercy found her mother in the kitchen with Harriet. "What are you doing, *Mamm?*"

Wilma walked over, and they embraced. "I'm so happy to see you. I'm making lunch for everyone before you go to Ada's place. I thought you might be hungry." Wilma moved back to keep preparing the food.

"Hello, Harriet."

Harriet smiled at her. "It's good to see you, Mercy."

Mercy gave her a quick smile back and then set her attention back on her mother. "I'm not hungry. Stop moving around. I need to talk to you."

Wilma grinned. "I've got things to do. We'll have plenty of time to talk later."

"No, Mother, I need to talk now."

Wilma sighed. "What's the matter?"

"I'm not going to Ada's place. I want to be alone. I need some time for myself. Stephen and the boys can stay there with Honor and their children."

Wilma took a deep breath and let it out slowly. "Your husband and children are staying at Ada's, and you'll go with them."

"I don't see why. Ada said you need silence, so I won't say a thing. I'll be out of sight. I'll only talk to you if you want to talk with me."

"It's not that simple, Mercy. Are you still having problems with Stephen?"

114

"Shh." Mercy glanced over at Harriet, who was busy filling the teakettle.

"Just stay with your husband," Wilma said.

Mercy huffed. "You don't want me here?"

"It's not that. It's just that we have arranged it."

"I'm not sleeping in the same room as my husband. I can't stand to be around him," Mercy whispered.

Before Wilma could react to that shocking statement, she heard loud screams coming from outside. She rushed to the window and saw that the four boys had taken off, exploring the orchard. "Is everything alright?" Wilma asked.

"Yes. They're just excited. I shouldn't have come," Mercy said before she left the kitchen.

Outside, Stephen noticed Ada's bandaged foot. "What's wrong with your foot, Aunt Ada?"

"Someone left a nail around and I stepped on it."

"Ouch. Well, all I can say is that you nailed it." He laughed and just at that moment, Mercy walked outside.

"What's so funny, Stephen?"

"I just told Ada she nailed it. She stepped on a nail, you see."

Mercy looked over at Ada's bandaged foot and then saw that Ada wasn't finding it at all funny. "Can you go and find the boys and tell them to stop screaming? When I went inside, I thought you'd watch them. See that they don't get into any more trouble, please?"

"Sure." He turned and headed off with his brother while Honor went into the house to find her mother.

Mercy walked over to Ada. "I'm sorry about your foot. That must've hurt."

"It did, a lot. You don't find Stephen's jokes funny anymore, do you?" Ada remarked, noticing the expression on Mercy's face.

CHAPTER 25

Mercy sighed. "I guess I don't have a sense of humor. He's always telling me that, but it's not just the jokes, Ada. Everything seems to get to me these days. Maybe that's my fault. I don't know."

Ada reached out, her hand covering Mercy's. "Every marriage has its seasons, dear. Some are sunny and warm, while others are cold as a winter's day and challenging."

Mercy breathed out heavily. "But what if this season doesn't pass? What if this coldness never goes away?"

Ada pursed her lips, thinking back to her own days as a young bride. "Have you tried talking with Stephen about how you feel?"

Mercy shook her head. "I don't know how to start. Every time I try, we end up arguing. Well, I argue, and he just sits there, which makes me even more cross."

"That's because communication isn't just about

talking. It's about listening too and understanding," Ada said gently.

Suddenly, a loud crash interrupted them, followed by shouts.

Mercy hurried toward the barn where the noise had come from. Ada followed as fast as she could with her bandaged foot. They found Stephen trying to calm down the boys. One of them had knocked over a ladder and broken a barn window in the process.

Mercy's heart sank as she took in the scene. Her first instinct was to lash out at Stephen for not watching them closely. But, as she looked into her husband's eyes, filled with concern and guilt, she felt a rush of empathy.

Instead of blaming him, she tried something different. "It's okay, Stephen. Accidents happen."

Stephen looked at her and took a moment before he spoke. "I'm sorry, Mercy. I should've been more watchful of what they were doing."

His older brother Jonathon said, "They're just being kids. Don't be so upset, Mercy. My brothers and I have broken a few windows in our time, haven't we, Stephen?"

"Yes, but that doesn't mean it's okay," Stephen replied.

"It hurt no one. That's the main thing. We'll organize to get a new window put in before we go home. There, problem solved," Jonathon said.

Ada stood there, hands on hips, looking at the mess. "Who's going to clean it up?"

"I'll do it," Stephen said.

"Let's go explore the orchard," Jonathon yelled out to the boys.

They all squealed and followed him as he headed off.

A squeak came from the house. "Mercy!"

Ada and Mercy looked around to see Cherish running at Mercy. Favor was walking behind her. Mercy ran to them, and they ended up in a group hug.

The girls got reacquainted for the rest of the day, catching up on news and sharing the latest gossip.

When Jared got home from school, he had a great time climbing trees with Mercy and Honor's boys.

Hope came over to see them and so did Joy, with her two girls. Then Bliss arrived, bringing a bunny-shaped chocolate cake. Wilma cut up the chocolate cake, Bliss helped with the tea and coffee, and then everyone moved to the living room.

CHAPTER 26

FOR A MOMENT, Wilma was delighted to have them all home again, but that was short-lived.

As it often happened, trouble soon began brewing when the six of her daughters were together.

"All that's missing is Florence," Hope said.

"Maybe we should call her," Joy suggested.

Wilma shook her head. "No. I don't think she'd come here. She's always busy."

Mercy's eyes flitted across the cozy living room, and her gaze landed on Cherish and Favor, who were giggling and whispering—a picture of sisterly warmth.

The two of them had always been close.

Joy sat there with her perfectly well-behaved daughters and that annoyed Mercy. Everything about Joy had always been perfect, and now she had perfect children.

Years-long resentments bubbled inside her. Everyone seemed so happy, even Bliss and Hope, despite them remaining childless. She would've thought they'd be despairing when Favor, who married after them, was now pregnant.

"Are your rabbits replacing children for you, Bliss?" Mercy asked.

A hush fell over the room.

Bliss opened her mouth in shock. "What do you mean?"

"Well, you've been married for ages now, so I'm just wondering if you're happy enough with just your rabbits."

"Of course, they don't replace children. I want to have many children. I'm confident I'll have children soon. It just hasn't happened yet. I try not to think about it because thinking will lead to worry. I have faith it will happen."

Favor immediately sympathized with her and then told Bliss, "I didn't think it would happen, but when I stopped thinking about it, it did."

Bliss smiled at Favor.

"I'm the same," Hope announced. "It will happen eventually. We're all so excited for you, Favor. If only you lived closer."

"You'll all have to visit me when the baby arrives."

"Yes, we're building onto the home and there will be room for everyone," Harriet said.

Everyone affirmed they would visit, and then Mercy's voice cut through the murmurs. "Cherish and Favor, why are you two staying here while Honor and I have to be with Ada and Samuel?"

Cherish wondered why Mercy was in a dreadful mood. "Mercy, we never intended—"

Mercy shook her head and interrupted Cherish. "It's always been clear who the favorite is."

Cherish's voice quivered, the sharp edge of the words embedding deeply. "That's not fair or true, Mercy. Remember, twice they sent me to live with Aunt Dagmar? They wouldn't have done that if I was the favorite."

Ada chuckled. "I'd say she was the trouble maker back then."

"Yes, only because you were trying to steal everyone's boyfriends. Anyway, look how that turned out for you. Coaxing Dagmar into leaving you the farm." Mercy crossed her arms.

The accusation hung heavily in the air, a tangible manifestation of the resentment that had simmered beneath the surface for so long.

Cherish's cheeks flushed. "I never coaxed Aunt Dagmar into anything. I didn't even know about the will until after she'd died."

Yet, Mercy remained annoyed. "That farm should've been divided between all of us. Even *Mamm* thinks so."

Cherish left the room and walked up the stairs to her old room.

Favor turned to Mercy. "Why are you being so awful? You've upset her. You always perceive yourself as the wronged one, always the victim. But it's you who's been spoiled, always wanting more, never content, and constantly comparing."

"No one asked you," Mercy snapped.

"Mercy, why are you bringing up things from the past?" Joy asked.

Mercy glared at her sister. "Choose a side, Joy. It's time the truth is acknowledged by this family!"

Joy blinked rapidly. "I'm not here to choose sides," she began softly, "but let's talk about what's upsetting everyone."

"The farm!" Mercy's voice cracked, barely contained fury and hurt glistening in her eyes. "Cherish got it all, and it should've been divided among us. Dagmar was *Dat's* sister."

Wilma sat there, sipping her tea. She had hoped that everyone would get along this time seeing they were older.

With a furrowed brow, Joy nodded slowly. "I think, morally, considering Dagmar had no children of her own, the farm might ideally have been shared..." She paused, meeting Cherish's eyes as she strolled down the stairs. "But it was her choice to make, and she chose Cherish."

Cherish sat down again. "I loved Dagmar, and she loved me. It was her decision, and I respected it. That's all I've got to say. I thought everyone was okay with that."

Favor looked over at Wilma, who had been quiet until now. "*Mamm,* did you say that the farm should've been divided?"

Wilma's eyes lingered on each of her daughters before she answered. "I might've thought it at some point," she conceded slowly, "but we can't dwell on what should've happened according to us. Dagmar made her choice, and it's not our place to question it. Why are we drudging up the past now?"

Cherish, taking a deep, steadying breath, replied, "I'm not. Mercy is. She's been insufferable since she arrived, judging and accusing."

Wilma sighed.

Joy shifted in her seat and faced Mercy more squarely. "Bitterness will get you only pain and resentment. It doesn't change the past and it will stop you from being at peace."

Mercy's lips turned down at the corners. "Always with the answers, eh, Joy?"

"Let's stop this right now. There's no need to be like this. Can't we all just be happy?" Bliss asked. "I should've brought some rabbits for us to pet. No one can be sad with rabbits around."

"Not a good idea. We don't know how Red will react to rabbits," Wilma said.

Mercy, visibly wrestling with the emotions that cascaded through her, remained silent.

The front door opened and Florence walked in. She paused, absorbing the heightened tensions and tear-streaked faces, immediately understanding something was wrong. "What's going on here?"

CHAPTER 27

Joy gave a brief description of recent conversations as Florence sat down next to Wilma.

"We cannot change the path that has been tread nor undo the choices of those who have gone before us," Florence began. "But what we can do is choose not to let past grievances dictate our future."

"Exactly," Joy agreed.

Florence, holding the gaze of each woman present, continued, "We're going to bury this right now. These seeds of discord should not be planted. I know what we need to do."

"What's that?" Hope asked.

"Let's share admiration and appreciation for one another, and let love be the foundation upon which we rebuild," Florence said. "We'll go around and each of us will share something that we admire or appreciate about each person present."

"Okay, who will begin?" Bliss asked.

"I will," Florence offered. "Cherish, I have always admired your kindness and unwavering compassion."

"That's two things," Mercy said. "Aren't you supposed to say one? If you give her two, you'll have to do the same for everyone."

Florence chuckled. "You're right, Mercy. I'll only do one. That's all that's needed. So for Cherish, I'll choose kindness."

Cherish's face beamed. "Thanks, Florence."

"Don't thank me. If everyone thanks everyone, this is likely going to take all day. Joy, I appreciate your gentle spirit. Mercy, your forthrightness is admirable. And Wilma, your unfailing love has always been the glue of this family." Florence continued around the circle.

The circle continued until it was Mercy's turn. She hesitated for a while before she spoke. "Cherish, I am sorry for being mean to you."

Cherish swiped a hand through the air. "Aw, don't worry about it."

"What I admire about you is how generous you are. I've always admired, even though I may not have shown it." Her gaze shifted to each woman sharing sincere praises.

As the circle concluded, a cathartic peace descended upon them. The vulnerability shared and acknowledgments offered had softly mended past hurts.

"This was a great idea, Florence. Thank you," Ada whispered. "I might add something. Love, understanding, and appreciation will always be the bridge over rough waters. Let them guide you through. Now, can someone get me a hot cup of tea? I'd get it myself, but I do have a sore foot."

"I'll do it." Harriet offered as she grappled with the depth of emotions and subtle tensions among everyone present. It was in this moment, perhaps for the first time, she found a sense of relief in having only one child.

CHAPTER 28

Everyone was in a more joyous mood as they said goodbye to Joy, Hope, and Bliss.

Wilma asked Mercy to check the mail; she came back with a few letters and a folded-over note.

"Sorry, I read it, Ada. It's for you, but I didn't know it was for you. It wasn't even in an envelope or anything."

Ada casually took it from Mercy. But as she read, her face paled. The note claimed to be from Samuel, declaring he no longer wanted to be married to Ada because of her 'heartlessness.'

Distraught, Ada's eyes welled up with tears, and she choked back a sob.

Wilma quickly snatched the note, reading it for herself. "Ada, take another look. Is this Samuel's handwriting?"

Wiping her tears, Ada examined the writing. "No... No, this isn't the way Samuel writes."

The realization dawned on them. "It's that boy again!" Wilma exclaimed. "But this handwriting... it's from an adult. The vegetable note was also from an adult."

Ada, her sorrow replaced with indignation, nodded. "We need to sort this out. Someone's helping Jared in these pranks, and we need to find out who it is."

Jonathon and Honor walked into the kitchen. "Hey, what's all the commotion?" Honor asked.

"Honor told me everyone was friends again. What's the latest upset?" Jonathon asked.

They told him about the notes Jared had been leaving around.

All Jonathon could do was burst out laughing. "There's never a dull moment around here."

Honor gave him a look that said, *'can you see how upset Ada is?'*

"Oh, sorry, Aunt Ada. But you know Samuel would never have said that, right? It had to be a joke. He's your husband, and he's always been devoted to you," Jonathan said.

Ada nodded. "I know, but everything has been getting to me lately, what with the nail in my foot, all the arguments, and so much wedding organization."

Honor put her arm around Ada. "Why don't you relax by the fire and put up your feet? There are so many people to help with the meal tonight. You don't need to lift a finger." Honor guided her out of the room to the couch, where she soon had a hot cup of tea and a cookie while she waited for the evening meal and waited for Samuel.

When Debbie came home, she learned about what Jared had done. She asked to see the note, and her heart plummeted with each word. "Where is he?' Debbie asked.

Wilma raised her eyebrows. "Didn't you see him when you came home? We thought he was in the barn."

"I just came straight inside. Gabe was out there, and he said he'd unhitch the buggy for me. I'll go see if I can find Jared."

CHAPTER 29

DEBBIE HEADED out of the house and saw Gabe rubbing down her horse.

She walked over and shared what Jared had been doing lately, handing him the note. She only told him because she'd seen how well he'd gotten along with Jared, so maybe he could get through to him.

Gabe's eyebrows furrowed as he read, his face a mask of concern. "Maybe he feels he's not getting enough attention."

Debbie nodded in agreement. "I have been busy with the wedding, but other than that, he gets all my attention. I'm not sure how to confront him. I mean, if he is upset or unsettled about me marrying Fritz, I don't want to upset him even more."

"Fritz might be able to talk some sense into him," Gabe suggested, trying to be helpful.

She hesitated, biting her lip. "I... I don't want Fritz to know just how challenging Jared has been lately.

Fritz is excited about being a father to Jared, and I don't want him to have second thoughts."

"Do you want me to have a word with Jared?" he offered.

Relief washed over Debbie. "Would you? I'd be so grateful. You're eating with us tonight, aren't you?"

He gave a nod. "Yes. I'll talk with him now and tell you later about how it went."

"Thank you."

When Debbie left, Gabe finished rubbing down the horse. Then he led the horse into the stable.

Jared was there, mixing the feed for the horses. "Hey Jared, can we talk for a moment?"

Jared stopped and looked up at him. "What did I do now?"

Gabe laughed. "What makes you think you did something?"

"This is the way it always starts. Someone wants to talk to me."

Gabe sat on a hay bale and patted the area next to him.

Jared walked over and sat down.

"Jared," Gabe began, "I know it might not seem like it, but being the oldest is a gift. Your mother will marry soon, and she'll have more kids, and that'll make you the eldest. I'm the oldest in my family, too, you know."

Jared looked up, surprised. "You are?"

Gabe nodded. "I am. And just like you, I had my moments of mischief. But with time, I learned that being the oldest meant more than just having younger siblings to boss around. It's a responsibility."

Jared scrunched up his face, considering. "But what if I don't want that?"

Gabe leaned forward, holding Jared's gaze. "It's fun. You'll always have someone to play with. They'll look up to you. And it's a privilege to be someone's role model."

Jared fidgeted with his shoelaces. "I don't want brothers or sisters. I like it just being me and *Mamm.*"

Gabe's heart went out to the young boy. He remembered the complexities of transitioning from being an only child to suddenly sharing what little attention he'd been given. "I get it," he said softly. "Change can be hard. But think of all the fun you'll have, the memories you'll make. And you won't be alone in this. Your mom will always be there, and so will Fritz. And you'll always have me as a friend."

Jared looked up, his eyes wide. "You don't live here."

"We can write letters."

"*Jah,* okay. I'm getting better at writing."

Gabe lifted the note he'd been given. "It seems so." He unfolded the 'Ada' note.

Jared looked over, and his face fell. "They think I wrote that?"

Gabe chuckled. "Nice try. If you didn't write it, someone wrote it for you. Anyway, I think you owe Ada an apology. I heard about the nail in her foot, the vegetable note, and now this."

Jared's lips turned down at the corners.

"Do you have a problem with Ada?" Gabe asked.

"She's always picking on me. The nail was an accident. I'm just a kid, and they left me to clean everything up."

Gabe nodded in understanding. "It can be tough when it feels like everyone's against you, and sometimes when we feel overwhelmed, we make choices that we later regret. But it's important to take responsibility for our actions, even if they were unintended."

Jared kicked at the loose straw on the ground, looking down. "I guess."

He placed a gentle hand on Jared's shoulder. "But remember, it's also okay to speak up when you feel you're being treated unfairly. If you tell them how you feel, maybe they'll understand better."

Jared looked thoughtful for a moment. "But they won't believe me. I've done too many things."

Gabe chuckled lightly. "Then it's time to show them the better side of yourself. One good deed at a time. And it starts with an apology."

Jared sighed. "Okay, I'll apologize. But only if she stops picking on me."

"Sounds like a deal," Gabe said. "Now, how about we finish up here and head inside for dinner? I'm starving."

CHAPTER 30

HOURS LATER, the remnants of the large family dinner were scattered across the kitchen. Empty plates, half-filled glasses, and crumbs told the tale of laughter, shared stories, and togetherness.

Wilma and Debbie moved together, clearing the table, washing dishes, and storing away the leftovers. The room, once filled with chatter, now echoed with the soft clinks and splashes of their cleaning.

Wilma, wiping down the counters, cast a sidelong glance at Debbie, noticing the furrow in her brow. "What's on your mind?"

Debbie hesitated, her hands submerged in sudsy water. "It's Jared," she began. "You saw how he acted tonight, right?"

Wilma nodded, remembering the boy's mischief: knocking over a vase of flowers, snatching food from plates, and teasing Mercy and Honor's boys. "He's a lively one, that's for sure. He apologized to Ada for the note during the meal. I think that's a good start. The other things he did during dinner were just him being excited to have other children there."

Debbie bit her lip, her gaze distant. "It's not just tonight. He's been acting out more recently. And with Fritz coming here soon, I'm worried."

Wilma dried her hands and turned to face Debbie. "You're thinking Fritz might not have enough patience?"

Debbie nodded, tears forming. "Fritz is kind and gentle, but he's also not used to children so much. Jared can be a handful. What if Fritz can't cope with it? What if he regrets marrying me?"

Wilma took a deep breath. "My dear, every marriage faces challenges. Every parent faces the task of understanding and guiding their children. Fritz knows Jared. He's spent time with him. And remember, he loves you deeply, so nothing will be a problem."

Debbie mumbled, "But he's never lived with Jared day in and day out. I just want our family to be harmonious."

Pulling back, Wilma held Debbie at arm's length, studying her face. "You must talk with him. Marriage is a partnership. You'll face these challenges together."

A shaky breath escaped Debbie. "It's just... overwhelming sometimes. Thinking about merging our lives, ensuring Jared is okay with everything, and adjusting to a new life with Fritz. Meanwhile, I've got the tea business. It's a lot."

From the other room, joyous squeals and the sound of playful banter filled the air.

Wilma, hearing the laughter, smiled softly and brushed a stray hair behind Debbie's ear. "Change always brings uncertainty, but you're ready for a new beginning. Trust in *Gott* and trust in yourself."

Debbie nodded. "Thank you, Aunt Wilma. I needed some reassurance."

The two women resumed their cleaning. "When is he coming?" Wilma asked.

"He said he'd be here tomorrow. He's heading to his mother's house first. Then he'll be here to see me."

"Ah, good. I'm sure that once you're together again, it will settle all your worries."

"I hope so."

Suddenly, a blur of youthful energy burst into the kitchen as a group of children stormed in, playing an animated game of tag. Little feet pattered on the wooden floor and giggles echoed as one child tried to tag another. In the midst of it all, they knocked a jar of jam off the counter.

Debbie lunged, catching it just in time. "Easy there!" she admonished, her heart still racing.

From the doorway, Honor's voice rang out. "Alright, you little rascals! Out you go! The kitchen isn't a playground." She herded them out. Coming back in, she raised an eyebrow at Wilma and Debbie. "Sorry about that. The boys have been wound up today. They're excited to be here."

"Thanks, Honor. It's just been one of those days," Debbie said.

Honor moved closer, looking at the remnants of the meal and the stack of dishes yet to be washed. "Do you need some help here?"

Wilma smiled, handing her a dishtowel. "There's always room for one more pair of hands."

CHAPTER 31

THE NEXT MORNING, Ada arrived with Harriet, Mercy, and Honor. The boys stayed with their fathers, and then all Wilma's daughters headed to Florence's house, leaving the older women to bake some bread.

"You know," Wilma began, expertly kneading a batch of dough, "It feels like ages since it's been just the two of us in this kitchen."

Sitting at the table, Ada chuckled. "Ah, Wilma, I've missed this since my foot was injured. I haven't been able to do a thing and I've barely got to talk with you in the last couple of days. The girls visiting Florence is a blessing in disguise."

Wilma smiled, her eyes crinkling. "Oh, I know they're having a grand time. Florence has always had a knack for keeping people entertained."

In another room, the repetitive swish of a broom sounded. Debbie, waiting for Fritz's arrival, kept herself occupied. Every once in a while, she'd glance outside, anticipating the sight of his horse and buggy approaching.

Debbie paused her sweeping, taking a moment to let out a deep sigh. The thought of Fritz's impending visit filled her with a rush of emotions.

Suddenly, the distinct sound of horse hooves on the dirt road became audible. It grew louder, closer. Debbie's heart rate quickened, and without a second thought, she dropped her broom and rushed to the door.

As she stepped outside, the sight of Fritz guiding the horse and buggy toward the house met her eyes. The winter's sun, now higher in the sky, cast a halo around him, making the moment seem almost unreal.

Fritz caught sight of her, and a wide smile broke across his face, mirroring Debbie's own joyous expression. The horse came to a stop, and Fritz swiftly descended from the buggy, taking a moment to pat the animal before turning his attention to Debbie.

The two met in a heartfelt embrace, the kind that speaks volumes with no words. "I've missed you," Debbie whispered.

"And I you," Fritz replied, pulling back slightly to gaze into her eyes. "Every moment away has felt like an eternity."

Debbie chuckled softly. "Come on, let's get you inside. Aunt Wilma and Ada are in the kitchen, and I'm sure they'll be delighted to see you."

As they stepped into the warm confines of the

kitchen, Wilma, hands covered in flour, looked up and beamed at him. "Fritz! It's been a while."

Ada got to her feet, and gave Fritz a gentle hug and then introduced him to Harriet. "How have you been?" Ada asked him.

Fritz, with his usual modesty, smiled. "Better now that I'm here with all of you. The journey was smooth, and it's always a pleasure coming here."

After a few more moments of pleasantries, Wilma suggested, "Fritz, have you thought about where you two will settle after the wedding?"

Fritz looked at Debbie, then back at Wilma. "We've discussed it a bit but have made no firm decisions."

"I had thought you'd decided you'll be living in the house that I offered you, but Debbie seems unsure. If you're going to be living in it, decisions need to be made fairly quickly."

Debbie felt a lump in her throat. Turning to Fritz, she said, "Why don't we see it now?"

Fritz nodded. "That's very kind of you, Wilma. We appreciate the offer, but before you offered that, I looked at another option."

Ada's lips turned down at the corners. "Well, is the other place locked in?"

Debbie felt caught in the middle and then repeated, "Fritz, why don't we look at the place Wilma's offering us today?"

He gave a nod. "We can do that."

"It's a sturdy home. With some love and care, I

believe it could be transformed into a cozy nest for both of you." Ada gave a nod.

Fritz grinned. "A nest? I'd like to have a look at that."

"Have some soup first. Are you hungry, Fritz?" Ada asked.

Fritz grinned. "Always."

With a plan in mind, Debbie heated Fritz some soup before they headed to their potential new home.

CHAPTER 32

Earlier that day...

The icy wind whistled through the Baker Apple Orchard. The four sisters, Cherish, Favor, Mercy, and Honor, walked side by side. They approached the grand boundary that separated their world from that of their stepsister, Florence.

As they approached Florence's property, the orchard transformed into beautiful gardens with sculpted hedges. The house itself stood tall and regal, a testament to modern architecture with its vast glass windows, white stone facade, and sprawling patio.

"Wow," whispered Cherish, her eyes widening. "It's like something out of a dream."

Honor nodded. "I never imagined Florence living in such a place."

Cherish added, "Neither did I. But she's always liked the finer things. Remember how she used to sneak those *Englisher* magazines into the house, hmm?"

Before anyone could respond, the front door opened, revealing Florence. Her Amish roots were clear, but she had embraced the *Englisher* way of life. Beside her was her young daughter, Iris, and in her arms was a tiny bundle—baby Chess. His face was peeking out from a soft blue blanket.

"Florence!" Favor exclaimed, rushing forward to embrace her. The others followed suit, the warmth of the reunion palpable.

Florence smiled. "It's been too long. Come in, come in! I've prepared some tea."

The interior of the house was as grand as its exterior. High ceilings, a majestic staircase, and tasteful decor greeted them. The sisters tried to mask their awe, but it was clear they were out of their element.

As they settled into the plush seats of the living room, Iris climbed onto Mercy's lap, chattering about her toys and friends. Chess, in Cherish's arms, cooed and gurgled, his tiny fingers grasping at her *kapp* strings.

After a while, the conversation shifted to Debbie's wedding. Florence stood up and disappeared for a moment, returning with a beautiful blue plain dress, neatly folded.

"I've put my heart and soul into this," she said, her voice soft with emotion. "I may have left the Amish community, but I still remember the traditions. I hope Debbie will like it."

Cherish touched the fabric. "It's beautiful, Florence. You've done a wonderful job."

Florence smiled. "Thank you. I wanted it to be special."

CHAPTER 33

THE SOUND of giggling and yelling filled Samuel's backyard, where the four young boys – all brimming with youthful vigor – engaged in a playful game of tag. Samuel and the boys' fathers watched, stepping in when necessary.

Samuel, catching sight of the large tree in the middle of the yard, had an idea. "How about we build a treehouse in the lower branches?" he suggested, pointing toward the sturdy boughs overhead.

"Oh, a treehouse? Can we really build one?" one boy asked.

Jonathon chuckled. "Well, we can certainly try."

They started gathering materials and tools for the plan, their excitement spreading joy in the air.

"Hold the plank steady, son," directed one father to his little boy, his hands guiding the youngsters as they worked together.

Meanwhile, the oldest boy found the allure of the

tall branches irresistible. His small hands clasped tightly around the rough bark, and he began his ascent, climbing higher and higher.

Samuel, spotting him, called out with a firm tone, "Come back down. That's not safe if you go too high."

But inches away from his targeted branch, the boy stole a quick, triumphant look downward and slipped.

A collective gasp enveloped the scene as he tumbled through the air, finally landing with a muffled thud on a bed of leaves below. The fathers and Samuel raced over.

Samuel, kneeling beside the boy, breathed a shaky sigh of relief at seeing no apparent injury. "Are you alright?"

Tears cascaded down his cheeks. The boy nodded, more startled than hurt, yet his pride was slightly bruised.

Jonathon enveloped him in a gentle embrace. "That was a scary moment, wasn't it? We have to remember to be safe and listen when we're told not to do something dangerous, okay?"

Finding him mostly unscathed, they showered him with reassurance and love.

"Boys," Samuel began, adopting a gentle but serious tone, gathering the young adventurers around, "Building and climbing are a lot of fun but we must all remember that safety is the most important thing. Do you understand?"

Heads nodded solemnly in response.

Samuel tipped his hat back on his head. "Perhaps we should forget the treehouse idea."

"No, don't do that," Jonathon said.

Walking back to the treehouse frame, Samuel mused. "Well, if we continue we'll have to take more care."

Jonathon tapped his young son on his shoulder. "Let's not tell your mother about this, okay? She'll only worry."

He agreed.

CHAPTER 34

THE RHYTHMIC BEAT of horse hooves formed a soothing backdrop as Debbie and Fritz made their way to the cottage.

"This is it here," Debbie said.

Fritz pulled up in front of the house. "So this was a rental property of Uncle Levi?"

"That's right, isn't it cute?"

"If by cute you mean small, then I agree."

Things weren't getting off to a good start, but Debbie was determined to encourage him to like the place. "A storm damaged it, but all the repairs have been completed now. Carter oversees all Levi's houses for Wilma now."

"That's good of him."

"Carter and Wilma are getting closer. It's nice to see."

They got out of the buggy and headed to it.

Fritz stopped in front of the house and had a good

look. "Well, it hasn't been painted lately. I thought you said that Carter was looking after things."

"It looks okay to me. I think it's structurally good. We can easily paint it. Actually, I prefer it to need painting because we can paint it any color we like."

Fritz then pointed out areas where the paint was peeling. "And the fence needs repair, too."

"Let's have a look inside, shall we?" Debbie asked.

Stepping inside, the wooden floors creaked underfoot, each groan telling a story of previous inhabitants. Then, they entered the kitchen with its mix of old appliances and cabinets that showed it had been updated at different times.

The bedrooms held the lingering imprints of numerous past occupants. The overall wear and tear throughout the cottage spoke to its history as a rental home.

Fritz, absorbing the details of every nook and cranny, finally broke the silence. "It's got character, but it would need a lot of work. The roof, the floors, the plumbing…"

Debbie nodded, biting her lip. "It might not be ready-made, but it's something. It's our start. The roof is fine, I know that much. Carter made sure that they repaired the roof after the storm. So, we don't have to worry about that."

There was a pause before Fritz, hesitatingly, said, "Actually, Debbie, there's something I've been meaning to tell you." She turned to him, puzzled by the sudden seriousness in his tone. "Before Aunt Wilma offered this cottage, I had already secured another house for us. It's in better condition, more suited for us to start our life together. I intended it as a surprise for after our wedding."

Debbie's eyes widened. "Why didn't you say something earlier?"

Fritz looked a tad sheepish. "I thought I might have, but since you didn't mention it..."

"I don't remember you saying a thing. We had that whole conversation about you wanting to pay something toward this house if we accept it. I talked to Wilma about it and everything."

"Sorry. I meant to tell you. Or maybe I wanted it to be a memorable moment, a surprise. But seeing this cottage and how small it is, it felt right to tell you now."

"Where will we live?" Debbie looked away, upset that he hadn't remembered such a vital thing. It just told her that, to him, there were more important things going on than marrying her.

The weight of this revelation hung in the air. With all its potential, the old cottage was a kind gesture from Aunt Wilma. Yet, Debbie couldn't insist upon living there if Fritz didn't want to do it.

"I genuinely thought I had mentioned the other house. With all the wedding preparations and my commitments at the mill, I must've lost track. It doesn't mean I'm not taking our future seriously."

Debbie turned back to him, her eyes searching for sincerity in his. "It's just...this whole situation has been overwhelming. Planning a wedding, thinking about where we're going to live, all while trying to navigate our feelings and expectations. Communication is vital, Fritz."

He nodded, his face reflecting his remorse. "You're right. I should've been more attentive. This is our future we're talking about, and we need to make these decisions together."

For a few moments, they simply stood there staring at each other.

Debbie finally broke the silence. "Let's see this other house you're talking about. But please, Fritz, no more secrets or surprises."

Fritz smiled. "Agreed."

With that agreement hanging tenderly between them, Debbie and Fritz departed from the cottage. Fritz guided the horse to the south, a gentle assurance in his eyes as he glanced toward Debbie, who still held a shadow of worry in her gaze.

"Is it far from here?" Debbie inquired.

"Not at all. Just a few miles. I chose it partly for its proximity to everyone we care about," Fritz explained.

CHAPTER 35

SEVERAL MINUTES ALONG, Fritz turned his horse and buggy onto a smaller road.

Eventually, a quaint, well-kept house came into view. It appeared larger than the cottage and exuded a welcoming charm with its fresh paint, well-maintained garden, and an overall air of being cherished.

Debbie glanced at Fritz, her expression softening. "Is this it?"

Fritz nodded, "Yes, it's not just the appearance, Debbie. I wanted our home to be a place where you'd be happy, where we could grow old together."

As they stepped down from the buggy and approached the house, Debbie took in every detail: the soft swaying of the curtain in the gentle breeze and the vibrant colors of the blooming flowers by the windowsill.

Fritz, sensing her silent contemplation, reached for her hand. "I may not get everything right, Debbie, but I always strive to make the right decision. This house is a step in the right direction. I didn't know Wilma was going to offer that other house."

"I understand. Well, let's go in."

Stepping inside, a cozy living room greeted them, its walls adorned with soft, comforting hues and an unlit fireplace that promised warmth in the winter months to come.

"The owner was an elderly lady looking to move closer to her children. She was keen on ensuring that the house went to a family that would appreciate and care for it," Fritz elaborated, guiding Debbie through the rooms.

Debbie, navigating through a swirl of emotions, found a smile curving her lips. She appreciated Fritz's effort and the depth of his intentions, even if they were not communicated in the best way initially.

"Fritz, it's beautiful," she murmured. "But you need to understand, it's not about the house. It's about us deciding together. I want to be included rather than kept in the dark. Now things are awkward with Wilma and that other house. If I'd known, I could've told her at the beginning when she suggested it."

"We discussed this already. There's no point going over it all again. If you were an employee, I'd fire you."

Debbie's mouth fell open. "You'd fire me?"

"In my business life, I don't have time to keep going over things that have already been discussed. It's a waste of time and I don't like my time being wasted."

"I'm going to be your wife, Fritz. You can't say things like that to me."

He looked away and she saw him clenching his jaw.

She looked up, locking eyes with him. "If I'm repeating myself, I'm just doing that because of how much it upset me. Now I have a problem with you saying you'd fire me."

Fritz lifted her hand, gently pressing his lips to it. "I'm sorry. I'm not normally like this. I'm just tired. I will include you in decisions, Debbie, as far as possible and as long as it's practical. Let's go outside. I'll show you where I plan to build the barn and the stable area."

The vast stretch of land behind the house, punctuated with mature trees and vibrant wildflowers, seemed to hold a promise of so many possibilities.

As Debbie and Fritz strolled hand in hand across the field, the lingering tension melted away, replaced by a tentative hope for the future that lay ahead.

Fritz, with an animated gleam in his eyes, began sharing his vision for the space. "Right over there," he pointed toward a slightly elevated patch of land, "I'll build the barn. It'll have a solid foundation and enough sunlight during the day."

He went on, detailing his thoughts about stable positions, the pasture for grazing, and potential spots for other outbuildings. There was an enthusiasm in his voice that made Debbie smile.

As she listened to Fritz's plans, Debbie imagined the life they could build here: lively animals frolicking around, the land bustling with activity. If God willed it, their children would run through the fields, their laughter mingling with the tranquil sounds of nature.

Stopping by a large, sturdy oak tree, Fritz turned toward her, his voice softer. "And under this tree, I envisioned a little picnic spot for us. A place where we can steal moments away from our busy lives, just you and me."

Debbie leaned into him, moved by his thoughtfulness. Her voice barely more than a whisper, she confided, "I can see it, Fritz. I can see our future here. But I need to be able to trust you to be open with me, to share things with me, good or bad, from here on out."

He pulled her into a tight hug. "I've promised, haven't I?" Fritz said.

"Thank you," she whispered.

Debbie nestled into Fritz, placing her head on his shoulder, and in that moment, all her concerns melted away. They lingered in the embrace, and she shut her eyes, immersing herself in the moment's tranquility. The memory of the moment under the oak tree, serene surroundings, and gentle breeze would stay with her forever.

CHAPTER 36

THE HOURS FLEW by as the sisters caught up with Florence.

Walking back to Wilma's orchard, the sisters reflected on their visit. The world Florence had chosen differed vastly from theirs, but at the heart of it, family and love remained constant.

"I'm glad we went," said Honor, breaking the silence. "It's good to see Florence so happy."

"Yes," agreed Mercy. "She's changed so much. She was always so grumpy when we were growing up."

That night, the dining table was alive with chatter and laughter. Ada and Samuel were at their home with their guests, so the only guest at Wilma's house tonight was Fritz.

Everyone was excited about the upcoming wedding, and talk of the future dominated the conversation.

"How do you feel about coming back home after being away?" Wilma asked.

"It feels right, especially with Debbie by my side."

The evening progressed with more shared stories, laughter, and an air of anticipation for what lay ahead. Then, Wilma brought up the subject of their future residence.

"Neither of you told me what you thought of the house." Wilma looked from Fritz to Debbie.

Debbie felt a lump in her throat. "We were going to speak with you about that afterward."

Wilma nodded. "Okay."

Jared, allowed to sit at the big table tonight, started talking to Fritz about birdhouses and what he thought about them.

Once the meal was over, Wilma sat at the table with Debbie and Fritz.

Wilma poured a fresh cup of tea for each of them, her eyes reflecting a gentle, inquisitive light. "Now, what did you want to talk to me about?"

Fritz and Debbie exchanged a glance, a silent agreement passing between them. It was Debbie who spoke, her voice gentle and cautious. "Aunt Wilma, first, we want to express our gratitude for your generous offer of the house."

Wilma inclined her head slightly, sensing the 'but' that was likely to follow. "You're very welcome, Debbie. But I sense there's something more."

Debbie nodded, carefully choosing her words. "It's a kind gesture, and we've thought about it thoroughly. But Fritz had already secured a house for us before your offer."

Wilma's brows lifted slightly in surprise, turning her gaze toward Fritz, who confirmed with a nod.

"I meant to surprise Debbie after the wedding. I didn't know about your offer, and I certainly didn't want to offend you, Wilma," Fritz said.

A small, understanding smile played on Wilma's lips. "Your happiness is what's important, that's all. I have a solution."

Fritz tilted his head to one side. "What is it?"

"I want to give the house to Debbie. A gift from Uncle Levi. She can do with it what she wants. She can rent it out and get some money coming into the house. A little extra never hurt anyone."

Debbie breathed a sigh of relief, and Fritz nodded. "Of course. I don't have any objection."

"Good. Can I ask where your new house is?" Wilma continued.

"It's not far from here," Fritz explained, offering a few details about the house and its location.

"We'll have you over for a meal as soon as we're settled," Debbie said.

Wilma's face broke into a smile. "Well, it sounds lovely. I hope it becomes a beautiful home for you both, filled with joy, love, and perhaps a few little ones running around in the future."

The atmosphere lightened considerably with that blessing, the weight of the conversation lifting.

Debbie reached across the table, placing her hand on Wilma's. "Thank you for understanding, Aunt Wilma. We were worried about disappointing you."

Wilma gently patted Debbie's hand, her voice warm. "My dear, you could never disappoint me. I want nothing but happiness for you and Fritz. Always remember that."

From there, the conversation shifted, evolving into more wedding talk, ensuring that the shadow of the house conversation didn't linger over the trio. They spoke of dresses, guests, and the fun atmosphere they hoped to cultivate on Debbie and Fritz's special day.

When it was time for Fritz to leave, he said goodnight to the others, and Debbie followed him out to the porch so they could say their own private goodbye.

CHAPTER 37

THE COLD WINTER air nipped at their noses and cheeks as soon as they were outside. A thin layer of fresh snow covered the ground, reflecting the moonlight and making the entire world seem peaceful and serene.

Fritz cleared his throat, the misty cloud from his breath mingling with the wintry surroundings. "Debbie, I wanted to tell you something."

She turned toward him, the soft glow from the house casting a soft glow on her face. "Yes, Fritz?"

He hesitated for a moment, choosing his words carefully. "I won't be able to see you tomorrow. Some urgent business has come up that I need to attend to."

Debbie's eyes widened slightly in surprise. "Oh? What's come up?"

Fritz shifted his weight from one foot to the other. "It's just some unexpected matters I have to sort out before our wedding. I promise it's nothing to worry about. I also have to have a last fitting for the suit."

Understanding flickered in Debbie's eyes, and she nodded slowly. "I see. Well, it's alright. I was planning on visiting Florence tomorrow to pick up the wedding dress. I'll be doing that in the morning."

"I won't get to her place until the afternoon," Fritz said.

They stood in silence for a moment, enjoying each other's company, the only sound being the soft whisper of the winter wind rustling the bare tree branches.

"I should go," Fritz finally said, breaking the silence. "It's getting colder."

Debbie nodded, pulling her shawl tighter around her. "Wait. Are you okay about Wilma's offer?"

He inhaled deeply. "I just wonder about the timing of it all."

"How do you mean?"

"Well, it's been years since Levi died, so I'm just wondering if she's giving you the house because she thinks our marriage won't work out."

Debbie gasped in shock. "Oh no. That would never have occurred to her."

He shrugged his shoulders. "You asked me what I thought about it and I told you. You said you wanted me to communicate better. Isn't that right?"

"Yes."

"Those are my private thoughts." Fritz smiled, leaning in to give her a gentle kiss on the forehead.

With one last lingering glance, Fritz made his way to his horse and buggy, leaving Debbie watching his silhouette disappear into the night.

CHAPTER 38

THE FOLLOWING DAY, everyone in the family was cleaning Wilma's house from top to bottom in preparation for the wedding.

Debbie had washed some clothes and on her way to the line, the gentle whinnies of horses reached her ears as she approached, but another sound made her stop in her tracks. She heard the animated chatter and laughter of her son, Jared. Jared had a day off school due to them making repairs to the one-room schoolhouse.

Peeking around the corner of the barn, Debbie saw Jared struggling with a long pitchfork, trying to move hay from one corner to the other. It looked quite comical, as the tool was so much bigger than he was. Gabe was there with him, trying to hide his grin but failing miserably.

"Ugh, this is impossible!" Jared dropped the pitchfork in frustration. "Why do I have to do this anyway?"

Gabe squatted down next to him. "You know, when I was your age, I had this job too."

Jared raised an eyebrow, skepticism evident on his face. "You're just saying that."

Gabe chuckled, shaking his head. "No, I'm not. I started doing chores when I was three."

Jared's eyes widened in disbelief. "Three? No way!"

Gabe nodded, a hint of mischief in his eyes. "Yep. And we didn't have these fancy pitchforks back then. We had to use our bare hands."

Jared stared at him, trying to discern if Gabe was joking. "Really?"

Gabe burst out laughing. "No, not really. But I started doing chores when I was three. It's a rite of passage in our community. Teaches you responsibility and the value of hard work."

Jared mulled over this for a moment before sighing. "Maybe you can show me how to do it properly."

Gabe grinned. "Okay, I'll give you some pointers."

Debbie watched as Gabe patiently instructed Jared, sharing tales of his own childhood mischief and chores. They laughed as they worked and talked. It warmed Debbie's heart to see someone relating so well to Jared.

"Hey, you two," Debbie said, stepping out from behind the shadows.

Jared ran over to Debbie and wrapped his arms around her legs.

She kneeled down, giving him a big hug. "You're doing a great job with that large pitchfork instead of the tiny one."

Gabe walked over, wiping his hands on his pants. "He's a quick learner. Reminds me of someone I used to know," he said with a wink.

Debbie stood up. "Thank you for helping him."

Gabe shrugged, a blush creeping up his neck. "It's my pleasure. He's a good kid."

"I'm going to tell Aunt Wilma I can use the big pitchfork." Jared ran toward the house.

"And you... are you ready for this next chapter with Fritz?" Gabe asked Debbie.

"I sure am. He's a good man. And after all that I've been through, I think I'm ready for some stability, for Jared and for myself."

There was a brief silence, filled only with the distant sounds from the house and the movements of the horses.

"What are you thinking about, Debbie?"

She smiled, feeling completely at ease with him. "Just thinking about life. It has a way of taking us on paths we never expected."

Gabe nodded slowly. "I know. I just... I sometimes think about the choices I've made, the paths I didn't take."

Debbie took a step closer. "Have you ever come close to marriage?"

He looked away, his voice barely a whisper. "Once. A long time ago. Her name was Leah. We were young, and I thought she suited me well, but then she moved away. We lost touch, and I never saw her again." He rubbed his jaw. "Not sure what happened to her."

"I'm sorry, Gabe."

He met her gaze, his eyes reflecting old pain and regret. "It's alright. I've made peace with it. It's just... seeing you so happy to be getting married, it brings back memories."

"Life is full of 'what ifs.' But we can't dwell on the past. All we can do is move forward and make the best of the present."

Gabe sighed, a small smile playing on his lips. "You always know what to say, don't you?"

She chuckled. "I've had my share of ups and downs. It's taught me a thing or two." They shared a quiet moment of understanding. "Promise me something, Gabe," Debbie said softly.

"Anything."

"Don't close your heart off. There's someone out there for you, someone who will value and cherish you as you deserve."

"Thank you, Debbie. I think I needed to hear that."

"It's getting late. I have to pick up my wedding dress after I hang out the washing. Wilma suggested that I hang it undercover."

"Yeah. It looks like it's going to rain. Want a hand?"

"No. It won't take me long."

"I better get back to work before Fairfax sees me taking a break."

Debbie nodded.

She lifted the basket, its content made lighter by the thoughts she was carrying from her conversation with

Gabe. Her fingers worked automatically, hanging the wet clothes on the line, while her mind lingered over the recent conversation.

Suddenly, a raucous voice broke through her contemplation.

CHAPTER 39

DEBBIE TURNED to see Cherish rushing over.

"Hey, Debbie. Let me help with that." Cherish grabbed the clothespin out of her hand.

"Thank you," Debbie said, passing her a wet shirt. "I appreciate this."

"Don't you have to get your wedding dress?"

"I do."

"Want me to drive you over?" Cherish asked.

"No. I'll walk."

Cherish looked up at the sky. "You sure? It might rain. Something on your mind? You seem a little far away. Dreaming of your wedding, are you?"

"I've got a lot on my mind." Her last conversation with Fritz still troubled her, but she couldn't share those thoughts with anyone.

"Go. We've got everything handled here. Don't worry about a thing. Today is for your preparations. You enjoy yourself. There's more than enough people to clean the house, even with Favor pretending to be tired and sick and whatever else."

Debbie laughed. "Don't say that. Being pregnant isn't easy sometimes. Just you wait and see."

"Yeah, I've been waiting. It hasn't happened yet. Well, are you going, or what?" Cherish started hanging the shirt on the line.

"I'm going now. Hopefully, I can beat the rain." Debbie set off to Florence's, the air growing tangibly heavier around her, hinting at the coming rain.

Florence and Carter's grand house soon appeared before her after she slipped through the wire fence that separated the two orchards.

The door opened to a comforting scent of freshly baked bread and lavender. Florence opened the door with baby Chess in her arms.

"He's adorable, Florence."

"He's less adorable today. He wakes up and cries every time I put him down. I'm stuck carrying him around."

Debbie laughed, recalling what it was like when Jared was a baby.

As Debbie stepped inside, her eyes were immediately drawn to the beautiful blue wedding dress, elegantly simple, hanging by the window. It was a work of delicate stitches and heartfelt labor, an intricate dance of tradition and subtle modernity.

"It's beautiful, Florence," Debbie whispered, her fingers lightly tracing the smooth fabric. "Thank you."

Florence nodded. "Every stitch holds a prayer for your happiness, Debbie."

Tears pricked at the corners of Debbie's eyes, and she leaned over and kissed Florence's cheek. "That's lovely. You've made my day."

"How about you hold Chess while I make us a pot of tea? I've got every flavor of your tea."

Debbie took the baby in her arms, and her heart melted. How she longed to have another baby of her own.

"So, what kind of tea do you want?" Florence asked over her shoulder as she entered the kitchen.

"I'm fine with anything," Debbie said as she followed.

After sharing a cup of tea and a light chat, Debbie carefully packaged the dress and made her way back home. As soon as she stepped foot into Wilma's house, the rain poured from the sky.

CHAPTER 40

DEBBIE STEPPED CAREFULLY into Wilma's home, cradling the soft bundle in her arms. The dress, delicately wrapped in tissue and nestled within a garment bag, was more than just fabric; it was a symbol of leaving her old life behind and starting anew.

She walked through the hallway and made her way up the stairs to her bedroom. With great care, she slipped the dress from the protective covering, holding it up to the soft afternoon light filtering through her window.

Gently placing the dress on a hanger, Debbie draped it across the wardrobe door.

Stepping back, she took a moment to admire it. Every stitch, every seam, whispered promises of a wedding day filled with love and commitment. Memories of her previous wedding drifted to the surface, hurried and somewhat impersonal. This time, things would be different.

This wedding wasn't a secret, and everyone she cared about would be there to witness her union with Fritz.

Her gaze lingered on the dress for a few more moments before a weightier matter began pressing on her mind: Wilma. The house. How to broach the subject? Taking a deep breath, Debbie left her room and headed to the kitchen, where she knew she'd find her aunt.

Wilma was busy arranging jars on the counter. "Wilma?" Debbie began hesitantly, her voice soft.

Wilma turned around. "Oh, you're back. How was Florence? Did everything go well with the dress?"

Debbie nodded, her throat feeling suddenly dry. "The dress is beautiful, Aunt Wilma. Florence did an incredible job."

Wilma's eyes twinkled. "I knew she would! She has a gift."

There was a brief pause, then Debbie took a deep breath. "Wilma, I need to talk to you about something."

Wilma's eyebrows knitted in mild concern. "What is it, dear?"

"It's about the house. The one you kindly offered me." Debbie continued, choosing her words carefully, "I'm not sure that Fritz is happy about you giving me the house."

"I don't think that's right. He said he was fine with me giving it to you, and who wouldn't want a bit of extra money coming into the household?"

Debbie didn't like awkward conversations, but she

didn't want any problems in the future. "He told me he was worried you offered it to me because you thought our marriage wouldn't work out."

Wilma gasped. "No!"

"Yes. That's what he said. Now I don't know what to do. Maybe he thinks it should go in both names, seeing we'll soon be a married couple."

For a moment, Wilma said nothing, studying Debbie's face. Then she sighed softly, her expression understanding. "Debbie, this is a gift to you from Uncle Levi. Is Fritz any relative of Levi's?"

"No, but…"

"As soon as I see Carter, I'm going to have him switch it to solely in your name. If Fritz has a problem with it, he can come and talk with me. If he says anything to you, just say that I insisted because of your Uncle Levi."

"Oh no. I mean, he didn't say he had a problem. Please don't mention it to him. I might've heard things wrong."

"It's a gift and you can't refuse or return a gift, Debbie."

"I don't know what to say. Thank you, Aunt Wilma. You're so kind." Debbie didn't feel any better because there was no resolution. Fritz would still think the same, and here she was stuck in the middle.

"Too kind, you say? Well, don't tell anyone. I wouldn't want to ruin my reputation." Wilma laughed.

Debbie laughed along with her, and then the two of

them hugged. "I'm going to miss this place and miss you all."

"You won't be far away. The door is always open, and make sure you bring Jared back to visit us. Ada and I love having him around. Well, Ada might need a little distance until her foot heals."

"Of course. Jared loves being here. He likes being with the horses and making things with Eli. I only hope Fritz is okay with us taking the house. He likes to do things his way."

Wilma reached out, cradling Debbie's face in her hands. "Life is too short to dwell on houses and properties. What matters is love and family. Anyway, the house will be yours soon, and it's a gift, quite different from a handout."

"I don't know what I would've done if you and Uncle Levi hadn't taken me in when you did. What would've become of me and Jared? When I was pregnant, I was even considering giving him up for adoption."

Wilma looked over at the doorway behind Debbie, and her face turned white.

Debbie immediately spun around, following Aunt Wilma's gaze.

Jared stood there with his mouth wide open. He'd heard every word.

CHAPTER 41

JARED JUST STARED at his mother for a moment before he asked, "You were going to give me away?"

Both women rushed over to him. While Debbie was searching for words, Wilma said, "Jared, sometimes when life throws us enormous challenges, we think about all possibilities. But when Debbie saw you, when she held you as a newborn, her heart was filled with love. She never could've given you up."

Jared stepped back. "But she might have."

Debbie kneeled down in front of her son, her own eyes glistening. "Jared, you've always been the most precious thing in my life. The moment I saw you, the instant I held you, I knew you were mine forever. Nothing can ever separate us."

Jared sniffled. "You mean it?"

Debbie pulled him into a tight embrace. "I mean it with all my heart."

Then outside they heard a horse and buggy and the yells of children.

"They're here." Jared turned and ran to play with his friends—Honor and Mercy's children—who had just arrived.

Debbie stood up and looked at Wilma. "That was awful."

"I know. I couldn't believe it when I saw him there. I would've stopped you, but it was too late. The words had left your mouth."

"I hope he'll be okay. The last thing I want is for him to feel unloved."

Wilma shook her head. "Don't worry about it. He's probably forgotten about it already."

The both of them walked to the window and looked out to see Jared running around with the other boys like he didn't have a care in the world.

But for Debbie, it was one more thing to worry about.

CHAPTER 42

WILMA'S HOUSE continued to be a hive of activity. Everywhere one looked, there were mops, dusters, and pails filled with soapy water. It wasn't just any cleaning; it was the thorough kind, the one where every corner was scrubbed and every surface polished until it shone.

Wilma, with her sleeves rolled up, led the charge. Ada was wholeheartedly throwing herself into the task despite her occasional grumbles about her foot. Even Ruth had come to help. The visiting daughters made the work feel like a fun get-together instead of a chore.

Mercy, having finished cleaning the windows, pretended to see a mysterious figure outside. "Oh my, who's that dashing gentleman coming our way?" she teased, squinting for effect.

Everyone rushed to the window, only to find one of the barn cats strolling around the yard. Laughter erupted once more. "Oh, a truly dashing gentleman indeed!" Ada quipped, giving Mercy a playful nudge.

Later, as they were all on their hands and knees scrubbing the floors, Honor playfully splashed some water on Cherish. "Hey!" Cherish exclaimed, feigning indignation. "Two can play at that game!" She retaliated, blowing a cascade of bubbles Honor's way.

Wilma, attempting to maintain some semblance of order, tried her best to scold the two but couldn't contain her own laughter. "If you two keep this up, we'll end up having a bubble bath instead of a clean floor!"

Cherish, seeing a spider web in the corner gave everyone a little scare. With a shriek, she pointed. "Look at the size of that spider!" Panic ensued for a split second before everyone realized it was just a small house spider.

Ada, catching her breath, said, "My heart! Cherish, one of these days your pranks will be the death of me. I thought it was a joke at first."

The sound of laughter echoed through the rooms as the women shared stories and teased one another. Mercy accidentally dropped a vase while dusting, but instead of getting in trouble, Wilma laughed and made a joke about her clumsiness.

Cherish couldn't believe the change in her mother. First, she had let a stray dog into her home, and now she was being nice when someone broke something. She had never seen this side of her mother.

Favor turned cleaning into a dance, twirling with

her mop and making the others giggle with her antics. Harriet scolded her and told her to slow down. Favor gently lowered herself onto a chair, pressing a hand to her forehead. "I think I need a moment," she murmured, her face a little pale.

Ada, throwing a suspicious glance her way, mumbled under her breath, "Seems convenient to take a break now."

Wilma, always the peacemaker, was about to chide Ada for her comment when Harriet, Favor's mother-in-law, came to her defense. "Now, Ada, let's not be hasty. Favor's carrying precious cargo, after all. We shouldn't begrudge her a little rest."

Ada huffed, "I just think—"

"But there's no need to voice every thought," Harriet interjected gently but firmly, ensuring that the mood remained light.

Cherish, spotting an opportunity for some fun, winked at Mercy and Honor. "Oh, I think I feel faint too!" She dramatically swooned, making everyone, including Ada, burst into laughter.

Honor rolled her eyes playfully. "You always were the dramatic one!"

Harriet stood by, smiling as she watched the scene unfold.

CHAPTER 43

As the afternoon turned into evening, the food deliveries started arriving. Daphne and Susan came to help and, along with Ada and Harriet, they were all occupied for the next few hours preparing for the next day. Ada did her best to stop Susan from sampling the store-bought cakes.

In the other room the group took a momentary break, sitting in a circle on the freshly cleaned living room floor. Mercy started a game of "Whispers," where a message was passed secretly around the circle. By the time it got back to her, "Freshly baked pies are delicious" had turned into "Fishy lakes hide dishes."

They all doubled over in laughter, the exhaustion of the day's work momentarily forgotten.

The day had been filled with celebration and cheer, with family and friends gathering to prepare for the approaching wedding. However, the atmosphere changed as Mercy gently took hold of Debbie's hand, leading her into a quieter corner for a 'talk.'

"Debbie," began Mercy, her face serious, "There's something I want to talk to you about. It's something I wish someone had told me before I got married."

Debbie looked at her. She wasn't as close to Mercy as the other sisters since she lived so far away. "What is it?"

Mercy took a deep breath. "Before you marry, you need to ask yourself something. Is there anything about Fritz that annoys you or something that you believe you'd like him to change?"

Taken aback, Debbie frowned, "Not really. Why do you ask?"

Mercy sighed, her gaze distant. "After marriage, any minor differences, any minor quirks that might seem insignificant now, can become magnified. They have the potential to develop into significant points of contention. I learned this the hard way."

A hint of doubt clouded Debbie's eyes. "But Mercy, no relationship is perfect. Surely, love can overcome such challenges?"

Mercy reached out, touching Debbie's cheek. "I'm not saying it can't, but love alone isn't always enough. Marriage is a melding of two lives, two sets of habits. It requires work, patience, and understanding."

A silence fell between them, the weight of Mercy's words sinking in.

Mercy continued, "I love my husband, but there were things I thought I could change about him or that he'd change for me. Some of those things have only become more pronounced with time."

Debbie swallowed hard, her voice barely a whisper. "Are you telling me not to marry Fritz?"

Mercy shook her head. "No, not at all. I only ask you to be sure. Don't rush in. There's still plenty of time to change your mind."

"I appreciate your concern, Mercy, truly. But it's also making me more nervous."

Mercy hugged Debbie tightly. "I don't mean to scare you, only to make sure you have your eyes fully open."

"Thank you. I'll keep what you said in mind."

Mercy smiled softly and hurried away.

With the house sparkling and the last of the chores done, they sat down together, sharing a light meal and more laughter, grateful for family and the moments that brought them closer together.

CHAPTER 44

JUST BEFORE DARK, Debbie sat on the porch thinking about what life would be like as Mrs. Fritz White. Despite being the busiest day she recalled in Wilma's home, now it had grown quiet. Quiet enough for her to settle in the old wooden chair and think about tomorrow, and all the tomorrows after that.

Soon, all her days might end like this, on the porch with Fritz by her side. She did hope he would take the time to enjoy the simple, quiet moments.

He always seemed to be in a hurry. There would always be breakfasts that they would share together before he left for work. Surely, over breakfast they would take time to share the small details of their coming day.

Even their shared chores were something Debbie had envisioned with delight. They would turn the mundane into treasured moments and shared memories.

She'd waited for this for so long and it was nearly here. It was hard to believe tomorrow would be her wedding day. Her first wedding to Jared's father had been totally forgettable. This one would be a wedding worth remembering, and she was determined to savor every small moment.

The sounds of laughter echoed through the orchard as Jared ran around, chasing after a butterfly. She looked over at Jared, pleased that he was old enough to remember this important day.

Suddenly, Jared stopped in his tracks, his young mind evidently grappling with a thought. He approached his mother, his eyes wide with curiosity. *"Mamm,"* he began hesitantly, "where will we be moving to after you marry Fritz?"

Debbie looked down into Jared's expectant eyes, a lump forming in her throat. She had hoped to shield him from the uncertainties for longer, but she had always promised him honesty. Taking a deep breath, she gently responded, "It's all been arranged. You'll see it soon enough."

Jared's brow furrowed in confusion. "What if I don't like it?"

"You will."

"Does it have trees?"

Debbie pulled Jared close, hugging him tight. "Yes, plenty of trees."

Emotions played across Jared's face—confusion, worry, and a hint of sadness. "I'll like it if you like it," he whispered, clinging to his mother.

Debbie kissed the top of his head, her heart aching at his words. "No matter where we go, as long as we're together, we'll be happy."

"But what about my friends? And the orchard?" Jared asked.

Debbie sighed, understanding his concerns. "Life is full of changes, Jared. But remember, new beginnings can bring new friends and fresh adventures. And the orchard, it'll always be a part of our memories. We can visit anytime."

Jared nodded, trying to appear brave, but Debbie could see the wheels turning in his head, the effort he was putting into understanding and accepting these significant shifts in their lives. She squeezed his hand, a silent promise of solidarity no matter the challenges they would face. "And you know," she added with a hopeful smile, "maybe we can start our own garden, seeing you love trees. You can choose what we plant. How does that sound?"

His face lit up. "Can we plant strawberries? And sunflowers?"

"Absolutely," Debbie agreed heartily, her own spirit lifting with Jared's improving mood. "Strawberries and sunflowers and anything else you'd like."

As they talked about all the possibilities that their new home might hold, from the garden they would cultivate to the animals they might keep, Debbie felt the tension from the boy's frame slowly dissipate.

"Let's go inside. It's only leftovers for dinner tonight because everyone's busy cooking for tomorrow."

"Can I have a peanut butter and cheese sandwich?"

Debbie nodded. "I don't see why not. Fritz is coming to get me later and we're having a talk with the bishop."

"About what?"

"About marriage," Debbie answered.

"Oh. Can I get that sandwich now?"

"Sure." They stood up and hand in hand, they headed into the house.

CHAPTER 45

THE DAY WASN'T DONE YET. The aroma of fresh cakes wafted through the kitchen, an intoxicating blend of vanilla, cinnamon, and chocolate. Flour was strewn across counters, and colorful icings sat in bowls waiting for their moment of glory. The atmosphere was a lively mix of laughter, banter, and the clinking of utensils.

Cherish and Favor worked side by side, mixing batter and pouring it into pans. Ada and Wilma were on decoration duty, their hands deftly creating intricate patterns on each cake.

After placing another batch in the oven, Favor stretched and let out a little groan. "I need a moment," she said, stroking her back, the subtle curve of her belly hinting at her pregnancy.

Cherish shot her a playful grin. "Ah, Favor! Just finding reasons to rest, aren't you?"

Favor laughed. "Well, growing a tiny human is exhausting work! You'll understand soon enough."

Cherish winked. "I can't wait to get pregnant so I can rest all the time. Imagine, an excuse to nap whenever and gorge on all the cravings!"

Wilma, swirling cream on a cake, chuckled, "If only it were just about naps and cravings! But, oh, the joy of holding your baby for the first time... it's all worth it."

Ada, piping delicate flowers on another cake, nodded in agreement. "Indeed. And the journey itself, despite the swollen feet and endless midwife appointments, is truly *wunderbaar*."

The women shared stories of weird cravings, baby kicks, and the overwhelming emotions of motherhood.

Ada paused for a moment, looking around at the vibrant scene. "You know," she began, her voice tinged with nostalgia, "this reminds me so much of the old days. Our mothers and grandmothers would gather in kitchens just like this one, preparing for weddings and celebrations. The laughter, the stories... It's heartwarming to see the tradition continue."

Wilma nodded. "Yes, it's like a beautiful cycle. We were once the young ones, eager and curious. And now, here we are, passing on stories and recipes."

The room fell into a momentary silence before Cherish piped up with a mischievous glint in her eye. "Speaking of traditions, any secret cake recipes you ladies are hiding?"

The room erupted in laughter once again.

WHEN FRITZ BROUGHT Debbie home after the meeting with the bishop, he walked her to the front door. They stayed sitting on the porch talking for a while, even though it was chilly.

Debbie pulled her shawl around her to keep out the wind.

"I wanted to tell you something before tomorrow," Fritz said.

Debbie held her breath. "Go on."

CHAPTER 46

Fritz took a deep breath. "It's about my mother. She won't be able to make it back to the wedding," he confirmed, his tone apologetic. "She's with Peter's wife. She's been really unwell with her morning sickness."

"Oh." Debbie looked down. There was an unspoken tension between her and Fritz's mother ever since they first met. They were like two contrasting melodies trying to find harmony, but always ending on a wrong note. She drew a deep breath, searching for words. "I thought you would've told me before now."

"I delayed telling you because I was hoping she'd be able to make it back in time, but she's needed there."

Debbie slowly nodded. "It happened so quickly for them, didn't it? Maisy got pregnant just after the wedding."

"It did. Sometimes, life has its way of surprising us." A hint of a smile crept up his face. "I hope we're as fortunate."

Debbie chuckled, the mood lightening a little. "What, you want us to be surprised with a mini version of Jared so soon?" she teased.

Fritz leaned back, the contours of his face highlighted by the light coming from the window. "If our child has even half the spirit and personality Jared has, I'll count us lucky."

Debbie leaned in, her fingers intertwining with Fritz's. "He is one of a kind."

The sound of a branch snapping in the distance jolted Debbie out of her thoughts. She turned to the source of the noise, squinting to see through the darkness. Suddenly, a rustling sound came from the bushes nearby, causing her heart to race.

"Fritz, did you hear that?" she whispered urgently, gripping his hand tighter.

He followed her gaze, his expression turning serious. "Stay here," he said firmly, standing up and scanning the surrounding area.

Debbie watched anxiously as Fritz cautiously made his way to the bushes.

"It's only me," a voice called out.

Debbie got up and stood on tiptoes. "Matthew? What are you doing out here in the dark?"

Matthew emerged from the shadows, a sheepish smile on his face. "Sorry to startle you guys," he said, rubbing the back of his neck. "I just wanted to catch some fresh air, you know?"

"You scared Debbie," Fritz said.

Debbie smiled weakly, still feeling on edge. "If you're looking for Krystal, she's inside."

"Oh no… no. Just taking a walk, stretching my legs. I'll head home now. See you both tomorrow."

As he walked away, Fritz turned back to Debbie. "Are you okay? You seem shaken up."

Debbie whispered to Fritz, "I'll see what he was doing. Stay here." She stepped off the porch. "Wait up, Matthew."

Matthew stopped walking and swung around.

"Tell me truthfully what you're doing here. Were you looking for Krystal?"

He shrugged and avoided looking at her. "I guess."

She felt bad for him, knowing what it was like to give your all to someone and have them not fully return it. She'd had such a relationship with Jared's father. "You must know by now that Jed and she are in a serious relationship. I'm sure they've talked about marrying, and he's staying here, and they—"

"I know all that, but it doesn't change my feelings. I can't switch them on and off."

"Maybe you'll meet someone else at my wedding."

He shrugged his shoulders. "I guess anything is possible. It's just that seeing my two brothers here with their kids makes me think of what I'm missing out on."

"You'll find someone. Just keep an open mind, okay?"

"Sure. Is that all you wanna say, Debbie?"

She wanted to talk to him some more, but she

glanced over at Fritz, who was staring at them with his arms crossed. "Yes. Good night, Matthew."

Matthew turned around and continued walking home through the apple orchard.

"Well, that looked very secretive," Fritz said when Debbie reached him.

"He's still heartsick over Krystal."

"You should concentrate on us," he said with a smile.

"I am. That's all I've been thinking about. I would've liked your mother here for the wedding too, but I understand her decision."

Fritz nodded. "It certainly doesn't feel right to get married without her."

Debbie didn't know what to say. After a silent moment, she said, "What are you thinking?"

"Nothing. I'm just sad she can't be here. I wonder if there's another way."

"We can't delay the wedding. We have arranged everything," Debbie blurted out.

His eyes opened wide. "I wasn't suggesting it. I just want my mother here since she's the closest person I have in the world. Seeing we're talking about my mother, I would've hoped that you could've developed a bond with her since you don't talk to your own parents."

He'd spoken as though he was accusing her for the rift between herself and her parents. He didn't understand her at all or care about what they'd put her through.

The surrounding air had changed, grown tense, filled with unspoken words. It was a quiet, still night, yet between Fritz and Debbie, a storm seemed to brew.

Debbie didn't want to start an argument in case it cast a shadow over their special day. They could sort out these small issues later. "I'm sorry," Debbie said. "I know how important your mother is to you. And I genuinely hoped we could've built a bond. But the circumstances haven't been favorable. Maybe over time, we can do just that."

Fritz took a deep breath, searching her face for something. "It's not just about my mother, Debbie. It's about us, our relationship, the doubts and fears that creep in. Why didn't you tell me you were such good friends with Matthew?"

Debbie stared at her husband-to-be. "I didn't think I needed to. Matthew's always been a friend to everyone in Wilma's household, not just me. I have so many friends. Do I have to write all their names down and give them to you?"

"I didn't mean that."

"I'm sorry. I'm just a bit tense," Debbie told him.

"I understand. But we're a team, Debbie. We should share everything, the good and the bad and the things we don't need to."

Debbie swallowed hard. She had to tell him exactly how she felt. She couldn't continue until she had done that.

CHAPTER 47

DEBBIE TOOK a deep breath and then didn't hold back. "That's the problem, Fritz. In the last few months, we haven't really talked about anything. You barely have any time for me when I call you. And you only write one letter to three of mine. Now you want to know who my friends are. It seems you should've taken an interest before now."

"I've been busy, and I've had to upend my whole life for you. It takes time. I've been thinking about you even though I haven't had time to talk. I'm surprised you'd say that. I give you as much time as I can. Any other woman would be satisfied, but you seem to hold everyone to a higher standard."

Debbie felt tears sting her eyes. "I'm sorry. It's just... sometimes I get overwhelmed by it all. This wedding, it's my second chance at happiness, at love. I want nothing or no one to jeopardize that."

Fritz gently cupped her face, forcing her to meet his

gaze. "Debbie, our love is strong. It has been tested, and it will be tested again. But we have something real, something pure. We must hold onto that."

She nodded, the knot in her chest loosening slightly. "You're right. I just... my past experiences make me overly cautious, maybe even paranoid."

"I understand," Fritz whispered, drawing her into his arms. "I do want to know who your friends are. I only want you to have friends who are doing the right thing and following the right path."

Debbie wasn't sure what he meant by that. "All my friends are doing the right thing."

"Well, I'm not sure you're correct about that. I have heard things about Matthew."

Debbie recalled Matthew's recent run-in with the bishop. "He's just young and trying to sort himself out. Everyone makes mistakes. He has a good heart."

Fritz drew back.

"Did I say something wrong?" Debbie asked.

"I hope you talk about me in such glowing ways."

Debbie was concerned about the way he was acting. She hadn't been aware of this side of him. Perhaps it was nerves about the wedding. "Of course I speak about you in nice ways, and I'll always stand up for my friends."

"We'll talk about that when we're married. You better get a good night's sleep. We've got a big day ahead of us tomorrow."

If Fritz was scared about the wedding and having second thoughts, he wasn't the only one. "Fritz?"

"Yes?"

"Do you think we're moving too fast?"

Fritz took a deep breath. "Not at all."

Debbie shrugged her shoulders. "I guess I just want to know that you're looking forward to being married as much as I am."

A smile spread across his face. "I've changed my whole life and everything in it just to be with you. The timing is just right."

Debbie felt a rush of warmth. "I feel the same. But I also feel this weight of responsibility. Especially with Jared, he's already been through so much. I want to make sure our new home feels secure to him."

"And it will be secure," Fritz reassured her. "He's a great kid. And together, we'll give him all the love and security he needs."

Debbie gave a small smile. "He's really taken a liking to you, you know."

Fritz chuckled. "I've noticed. I'm fond of him too. Anyway, it's getting late, and tomorrow waits for no one. I should go."

Debbie nodded, understanding, but not quite ready to let him go. They walked together to where Fritz's horse and buggy were waiting. The horse neighed softly at their approach, its breath fogging slightly in the cool night air.

Fritz took a moment to pat the horse, his hands automatically checking the harness and ensuring everything was secure. He then turned to Debbie, taking both her hands in his. "Remember, no matter what, we're in this together. I am just as committed to this marriage as you are, and I look forward to every crazy, beautiful, challenging part of it."

The sincerity in his eyes made Debbie's heart swell, chasing away the last shreds of doubt. "I'll see you in the morning," she said.

With a last squeeze of her hands, Fritz climbed into the buggy. He gathered the reins and, with a skilled flick of his wrist, set the horse into motion.

Debbie watched as the buggy started down the driveway, the wheels crunching softly on the gravel.

She stayed there, bathed in moonlight, listening to the fading sound of the horse's hooves, feeling the rightness of the world in that moment. They had challenges ahead, but there was a promise in the night—a promise of commitment, love, and a shared future.

CHAPTER 48

As soon as Debbie walked back into the house, Cherish jumped in front of her. "Debbie, tonight, Favor and I will sleep in your room," she declared in a tone that left no room for argument.

Debbie raised an eyebrow. "Oh, is that so?"

Cherish nodded emphatically. "Yes! We'll stay up all night, sharing stories, eating snacks, and it'll be fun. It's a tradition in the family, you know? And then everyone's coming in the morning to help you get ready. Let me see, there'll be Christina, Joy, Hope, Bliss, Krystal, and Florence. And of course, Honor and Mercy. Oh, I hope I haven't left anyone out."

Favor, her hand gently resting on her rounded belly, chuckled. "I've never heard of such a tradition, Cherish. I'm okay with staying in Debbie's room, but I'm not sleeping on the floor."

Cherish rolled her eyes playfully. "Well, it's a tradition that starts from now. And no problem because I'll drag some mattresses in. What do you say, Debbie? Let's make your last night as a single woman one to remember."

Debbie laughed, her heart warmed by Cherish's idea. "Alright, alright, I'm in. But don't keep me up too late. We have a big day tomorrow."

"I might just fall asleep at any time," Favor admitted, her eyes droopy. "This little one inside keeps me up at odd hours, and I'm always so tired."

Jared, who had been listening to the entire exchange with wide eyes, tugged on Debbie's dress. "Can I sleep in your room too, *Mamm?* I want the snacks."

Cherish kneeled down to his level, giving him a gentle smile. "Sorry, Jared, but tonight it's a girls-only thing. But don't worry, we'll have another sleepover just for us soon, before I go home. Deal?"

Jared's face fell, but he nodded, understanding. "Okay, but can you not eat all the snacks?"

"We'll leave some for you, okay?" Cherish said with a laugh.

Once they'd set the mattresses down and decided who would sleep where, they started braiding each other's hair. Cherish had come prepared with a basket of pretzels, dried fruits, and some sweet baked goods. And she sneaked some cupcakes that were meant for the wedding feast.

They went into Krystal's room to get her, but she was fast asleep, so they left her there.

Once settled in the room, Debbie was delighted to have company. She knew she would get very little sleep, but she was fine with that. "This wedding means so much to me. My first marriage... it was nothing like this. It was hasty, hidden, a secret."

"We remember when you came here, and we found out you were pregnant, but you never told us about the marriage until later."

"I couldn't tell anyone. I think he intended to tell everyone the day that he died, but I'll never know."

"He would've. Of course he would've. He couldn't have kept it a secret forever," Favor said.

"I know, but nothing has ever come easily for me. I'm not sure why."

"But this time, it's different, Debbie. You're surrounded by so many friends and we all just want the best for you," Favor said.

Debbie nodded, drawing in a deep breath. "Yes, it is different. But," her voice wavered, "what if Jared's grandparents decide to come? Or worse, my parents? What if they try to cast a shadow over the day? That will be terrible."

"Then we face it together. You're not alone in this, Debbie. If they come, we'll make sure they don't ruin your day," Cherish said.

The stories eventually turned to love, and Cherish asked Debbie about her feelings for Fritz, resulting in laughter and whispers.

As the early morning hours approached, a comfortable silence enveloped the room. Favor was already fast asleep. Cherish leaned over and planted a kiss on Debbie's forehead. "I'm so happy for you."

Debbie smiled, her heart full. "Thank you. I'm glad we did this tonight. I just would've worried all night that something would go wrong tomorrow."

Cherish looked over at the clock. It was after one. "You mean today."

"Oh yes. We better get some sleep. I want to look my best."

Cherish snuggled under her quilt on the mattress closest to the door. They didn't take long at all to drift into a peaceful sleep.

CHAPTER 49

THE SOFT CHIRPING of birds and the distant murmurs of conversation drifted through the slightly ajar window, causing Debbie to wake.

The room was filled with the rhythmic breathing of Cherish and Favor, who had slept in the room with her.

Then she remembered what day it was.

It was her wedding day.

Today, she was to become one with Fritz, entwining their paths into a shared journey.

She unwound herself from the cocoon of comfort provided by her quilts, ensuring that she did not disturb the slumber of her friends. Her feet, barely making a noise against the floor, carried her to the window. Looking out, she saw people hurrying about.

Men moved with a practiced ease, unloading wooden benches from the community's wagon. They were moving the furniture out of the living room and moving the benches in. There were even people repairing the barn's window.

A stone's throw away, women were coming and going, bringing more food into the house.

With appreciation and excitement, Debbie quietly thanked the Lord for the day, the community, and all the love surrounding her.

There was a soft knock on the door. Debbie opened it to see Florence. "Sorry I'm so early," Florence said.

Debbie blinked heavily, trying to wake herself up a bit more. "I didn't expect you to be here at this hour."

"I just want to make sure the dress is right. I want to iron it."

"Thanks." Debbie reached forward, took the dress off the peg, and handed it to her while it was still on the hanger.

Florence glanced at her two half-sisters who were fast asleep. "What time did you get to bed?"

"I'm pretty sure it was after one."

As soon as Florence left, Ada and Wilma squeezed their way into the room.

"It's a big day for you," Ada said.

Then Krystal poked her head around the door. "Hey, I wasn't invited here last night."

"We looked in your bedroom and you were fast asleep," Debbie told her.

"You could've woken me up."

"Last time I did that, you threw something at me."

"Okay. I'll let you off the hook this time." Krystal

twirled her *kapp* string between her fingers. "You coming down for breakfast?"

Debbie put a hand over her stomach. "I don't think I can eat anything."

"You should try to eat something," Wilma insisted. "We don't want you to faint."

Cherish sat upright, still looking half asleep. "I'll eat."

Everyone laughed.

"What's going on?" Favor said as she slowly sat up. "What time is it?"

"It's time for you to all get dressed and come down and have a quick bite to eat. It'll only be cereal. There'll be plenty to eat later. C'mon now," Wilma said.

Several minutes later, they were all downstairs eating cereal and drinking juice when a teenage boy entered the kitchen.

"Sorry, I knocked, but no one came."

Wilma walked over to him. "Everyone's coming and going today. What can I do for you, David?"

"I have a note for Debbie."

Wilma took the note from him and handed it to Debbie. When Wilma turned around to ask who it was from, David had disappeared.

A collective curiosity hung in the air as Debbie gently unfolded the note and hastily allowed her eyes to scan the words.

As Debbie read it, the color left her face.

"What does it say?" Ada asked.

"It's...it's from Fritz," she whispered, her voice

barely a breath amidst the stunned silence, "He's gone...he can't...the wedding..."

A heavy silence blanketed the room.

Through the silence, Cherish asked, "He can't go through with the wedding?"

Debbie froze as the enormity of what she had just read sank in. The room, which moments ago had been filled with joy and excitement, was now thick with shock and sorrow.

Ada stood up and plucked the note from Debbie's hand. "Hold on a moment. This doesn't seem right. Could this be one of Jared's pranks? He's done two notes already. It seems this is a third."

Debbie was relieved when she realized what had happened.

"Why would Jared do such a thing?" Krystal asked. "He's not a mean kid."

Debbie bit her lip, recalling Jared overhearing that she'd considered adoption when she was pregnant. "He was upset with me recently. Jared did this for sure."

Ada looked around, trying to bring some order to the chaos. "First, we need to sort this out. Has anyone seen Jared?"

The fright of the note and the realization that Jared wrote it caused Debbie to burst into tears.

CHAPTER 50

Krystal put her arm around Debbie. "It's all right. It's not Fritz's writing, is it?"

"It might be if he was rushed, but I'm not sure. No, it can't be. Why would Jared do this to me?"

"Because he thought it was funny, or because he didn't know it would upset you so much," Wilma told her.

A flurry of activity ensued as Cherish and Favor searched for Jared while everyone else stayed back to comfort Debbie.

Harriet, who had been standing back silently, moved forward and handed Debbie a handkerchief. "Now, let's not assume the worst. We don't know the full story yet, and we'll sort it out."

Debbie tried to compose herself, dabbing at her eyes with the borrowed handkerchief. The mixture of emotions was overwhelming: a blend of relief that Fritz hadn't abandoned her, concern over what Jared might be feeling, and frustration at the disruption of what should have been the happiest day of her life.

Then she thought about her recent interactions with Fritz. "It could be true. Fritz's mother isn't coming and maybe he wants to wait until she can be here."

"Jared did it. It's a big change in his life, so he must be a little scared about it," Wilma said.

Ada's lips pressed together. "You'll have to think of a firm punishment for him for doing this. This isn't just about vegetables, and it's worse than the note he gave me that Samuel no longer wanted to be married to me."

"Not today, Ada. Let Jared be happy to see his mother getting married," Harriet told her.

"I didn't mean today, Harriet. But at some point, the boy's got to learn right from wrong."

A further weight pressed on Debbie's shoulders. She was a bad mother. She must've been doing everything wrong.

As time passed with no sign of Jared, anxiety wove its way back into the room. Florence reappeared, holding the freshly ironed dress, her eyes questioning the tension-filled atmosphere. "What's happened?"

They filled her in quickly, and Florence offered her opinion. "Jared's behavior might be his way of expressing fear or uncertainty. Big changes, such as weddings, can unsettle children, especially if they've faced instability before."

Debbie's heart clenched at the reminder of Jared's past—the little boy had indeed endured a lot. Maybe this was his way of acting out, of voicing his insecurities in a world that was changing around him. Again, it was her fault for her son having insecurities. "Hopefully, once Jared has a father, things will change for him."

"Definitely," Ada said.

The sound of hurried footsteps announced the return of Cherish and Favor, out of breath and with Jared in tow.

"There you are!" Debbie said. "Jared, I want you to tell me the truth. Did you write this note?" She held it out to him and he looked at it.

After a moment, he looked up at his mother. "Nope."

"Take a closer look." Ada grabbed the note from Debbie and held it right under Jared's nose.

Jared shook his head. "I said I didn't do it."

"We need the truth, Jared. It's important," Wilma urged. "We all know it was you, so you might as well admit it. Your mother is dreadfully upset right now. Maybe you didn't actually write it, but you got someone to write it for you, hmmm?"

"The truth," Ada insisted, glaring at him.

"Yes, we need the truth for your mother's sake," Wilma repeated.

Jared looked up and met Wilma's eyes. "Okay. I did it." He went to run away, but Ada grabbed his shirt.

"But why, Jared?" Debbie probed, trying to keep the edge out of her voice. "You're not in trouble if you just tell me why you did it."

"Is it because of what you overheard your mother say?" Wilma asked.

He hung his head and then looked up at Debbie. "I don't want you to give me away, *Mamm.*"

Debbie's heart broke right there. Kneeling down to his level, she pulled him into a tight hug. "Oh, Jared. That's not true. You misunderstood. You're not going anywhere. You're my family. I'll never give you away."

"You'll have a mother and a father, Jared. The only place you're going is to a new house," Wilma said, blinking back tears.

Ada stood there, shaking her head and everyone else was silently looking on.

Jared sniffed as though he was going to cry.

"It's okay," Debbie told him. "Now I have to get ready for my wedding, and you have to put on your Sunday best. Go up to your room and get changed. I've got your clothes on the hanger waiting for you."

Jared turned and ran.

CHAPTER 51

DEBBIE STOOD up and gulped as she faced the women. "I couldn't punish him. He was just scared."

Ada looked up at her. "You did the right thing. Harriet is right, today is not a day for punishments."

Florence clapped her hands gently. "Alright, everyone. We've had our crisis, and now we have a wedding to put on. Debbie, finish getting dressed. We'll take care of Jared and make sure everything is set up."

Debbie, feeling steadier and fortified by the love surrounding her, nodded. She took a deep, steadying breath and reached for her wedding dress.

As Debbie stepped into her dress, a symbol of her transition into a shared life with Fritz, she felt the pieces of her world clicking into place.

Looking out the window at all the people milling about, she looked for Fritz because she knew her heart would settle at the sight of him.

◠

AN HOUR LATER, as Debbie descended the stairs, she was met with all the smiling faces of the people she loved. This wasn't the family she'd grown up with; it was the family she'd chosen, and that had chosen her.

They were all there to celebrate her and Fritz.

She looked around for Fritz, and there was no sign of him.

Later, she'd tell him what had transpired that morning, and they'd laugh about Jared's note, but now wasn't the time to tell him that story. She'd leave it a day or two.

Fritz had been meant to meet her at the bottom of the stairs, but she couldn't see him anywhere. She waited a minute or two and then couldn't wait any longer. She had to sit down.

Each step she took toward the bishop was a reminder of the journey they had embarked upon together, with all its trials and triumphs. She looked over at Jared and saw him wearing a huge smile.

The bishop nodded toward a chair at the front and she sat down.

The air in Wilma's home grew thick with concern. Debbie sat as if frozen, the fabric of her dress feeling like the only thing holding her together. The murmurs around her seemed to come from a distance as she turned toward the bishop. "Where is Fritz?" Debbie whispered.

"I'm sure there's a good explanation, Debbie." The

bishop called a man over and he whispered to him. The man then hurried out of the house.

Fifteen minutes later, with still no sign of the bridegroom, the room was buzzing with restless guests. Their whispers seemed to grow louder with every passing minute.

The man who'd been sent off by the bishop came back and signaled to the bishop to meet him at the door. The two men had a whispered conversation.

All the while, dark and gloomy thoughts played over in Debbie's mind. Was that note from Fritz? Had he changed his mind?

The next thing Debbie knew, the bishop sat down next to her. It was no secret something was wrong. It was written all over the bishop's face.

"He's not coming, is he?" Debbie's voice quivered, the words tasting bitter as they slipped out.

The bishop's face was full of empathy, his expression doing little to cushion the blow as he locked eyes with Debbie. "We got in touch with his brother. Peter told us Fritz is on his way to join him and his mother. He also said Fritz sent you a note telling you he wasn't coming."

Debbie sat there in shock. Her hand went to her mouth as her body went cold.

The note—it was from Fritz.

"I'm sorry, Debbie," the bishop said.

Debbie had no answer, so she just sat there trying to make sense out of everything. She'd been rejected and not only that, she'd been publicly humiliated.

The bishop looked over his shoulder at the guests. "Shall I tell everyone to go home?" he whispered to Debbie.

"No," Debbie whispered back. "Let them stay and eat. There is no reason to waste all this food."

He nodded. "I'll make an announcement."

"Please do."

The bishop got to his feet. "Seems like there will be no wedding today. You are all welcome to stay and enjoy the food and have fellowship with one another."

Ada and Wilma rushed forward to Debbie, full of questions.

"He's left town," she said to them as they crouched down in front of her.

The living room, once a sanctuary of joy and antici-pation, now seemed to close in on Debbie. Each whis-per, each sympathetic or curious glance, was a piercing reminder of another rejection.

Jared walked over to his mother. "Where's Fritz, *Mamm?*"

"You didn't write that note, Jared?" Debbie asked.

"No."

Ada frowned. "But why did you tell us that you did?"

Jared shrugged. "I didn't want to get into trouble again."

Debbie held her head in her hands. Her life was a mess and Jared was suffering because of it.

"You're not alone," Ada whispered to Debbie.

Debbie sniffed back her tears and put her arms out

for Jared. He ran into her arms. "I'm sorry, Jared. I shouldn't have blamed you for something you didn't do. The note was from Fritz and now I won't be marrying him."

"Are you okay with everyone being here?" Ada asked.

"Let everyone eat and be happy," Debbie said. "There's plenty of food."

"No one will feel like celebrating, but someone's got to eat all this food. It won't keep." Ada sighed loudly.

Florence stepped forward. "Debbie, do you want to come to my house for a while?"

"Thanks, Florence, but no. I'll stay here. Wilma, can you thank everyone for coming?"

"Me?" Wilma asked.

"I'll have Samuel do it," Ada whispered.

A few minutes later, Samuel addressed the crowd. "Debbie wants to thank everyone for coming here today. Life throws us unexpected curves, and it's in these moments we embrace our community's true strength. Today, we rally around Debbie. While this isn't the celebration we anticipated, it is a coming together to show our unity. Let us stay and fellowship together as we give thanks for what *Gott* provides for us."

The atmosphere shifted as the people in the crowd absorbed Samuel's words.

Debbie, feeling the collective strength and acceptance of her community, found the courage to stand. "Thank you," she managed to say to Samuel.

As people moved out of the living room, some gathering in small groups to pray, others arranging themselves to provide any necessary support, Debbie felt the warmth of her chosen family around her. They wouldn't let her navigate this heartache alone. In that moment of vulnerability, Debbie understood — this was what community meant. This outpouring of unconditional support was the fabric of their Amish life.

Debbie looked down at her dress as all her closest friends gathered around her. "I'll change out of this and come back down."

"No one expects you to do that. Stay in your room, or I'll take you somewhere," Mercy suggested.

Debbie forced a smile. "It's fine. He's changed his mind. I just need to rethink what I will do with the rest of my life. I thought I knew my future, but now I don't. It's not the first time this has happened so it's likely not the last time."

"Can I go play?" Jared asked.

"Of course you can."

"Before you go, Jared, I'm sorry for thinking you wrote that note," Debbie said.

"I am too, Jared. Will you forgive me?" Ada asked.

Jared nodded and gave her a smile before he ran to play outside with his young friends.

CHAPTER 52

As DAY TURNED INTO NIGHT, the guests eventually departed. Wilma sat with Debbie and all her daughters were there, also surrounding Debbie.

"Everyone said for you to keep their gifts," Wilma told Debbie. "They will come in handy whenever you're ready to move into your cottage."

"Oh no. I'll have to return them."

"No. Gifts are gifts," Ada insisted.

"That's so nice of everyone."

"Why don't you open them now?" Cherish suggested.

"I can't. Maybe tomorrow."

At that moment, Jared walked into the kitchen holding an awkwardly wrapped gift. "I made this for you, *Mamm.* It's for our new home, but Aunt Wilma said we can still use it here."

"Thank you." Debbie took the gift from him and

unwrapped it. "It's a large birdhouse. I've never seen a better one."

"Do you love it?" Jared asked.

"I do. Let's find a tree to hang it in tomorrow." She put her arms out and Jared ran into them. "Do you understand that I'm not marrying Fritz now?"

"Yes."

"Are you upset? I know you were looking forward to having a father," Debbie asked.

"I'm not upset. Now you can marry Matthew."

Everyone laughed, and Debbie managed a smile. "I don't think that will ever happen."

LATER THAT EVENING, Honor sent Ada and Wilma out to the porch for a well-deserved break while others cleaned up. They sat with Red sprawled out in front of them.

"Ah, Wilma. What a day we've had."

Wilma nodded as she stroked Red with her foot. "I know. Debbie is coping so well. I'd be a total mess if that had happened to me. I probably wouldn't come out of my room for a week."

"I know, but I can't help thinking that we were right about Fritz all along."

Wilma nodded. "I agree. His reputation will be ruined now. I don't think any woman will agree to marry him when they find out what he did to Debbie."

"Maybe he has chosen not to marry."

"Possibly. We never found out who was helping Jared with those notes."

"No, but we will. I've got someone in mind," Ada said.

Wilma looked over at Matthew, who was helping Gabe and Jed take down the lights and the heaters. "Me too. It's hard to believe it all came together after the shock of Fritz leaving Debbie like that."

"Life has a way of surprising us, Wilma. We think we're just putting together a wedding, but really, we're giving the community a chance to come together, and strengthening the bonds that hold us all."

The two women shared a comfortable silence, each contemplating the weight of the day's events. Around them, the younger ones continued to move with purpose, cleaning and restoring order.

"You know," Wilma started, breaking the silence, "having all my girls here, seeing them helping Debbie, it's given me a sense of peace. It's like we're witnessing the threads of our teachings and love finally coming together. I mean, Mercy has her moments, but she has a good heart."

Ada nodded, understanding the depth of her friend's emotions. "The young ones are waiting for children or for their children to grow up. We're here for our families when they need us. To advise them."

"How about that birdhouse?" Wilma asked. "Was that the best one you've ever seen?"

Ada laughed. "It was nearly worth getting a nail in my foot just to see it. Well, not really."

"Ah, I'll miss Jared and Debbie living with me if they ever move to that cottage."

"I don't see that happening. You've always had a full house. Maybe Jed will move in once he marries Krystal."

Wilma grinned. "Maybe. I do hope Debbie will find a nice man. One who will treat her and Jared properly. That's all she wants. Is that asking too much?"

"Not at all, Wilma."

As the night deepened and the home quieted, a sense of fulfilment settled in their hearts. The failed wedding celebration had become an affirmation of faith and community.

CHAPTER 53

THAT NIGHT, Debbie's room hosted all of Wilma's daughters, along with Bliss and Krystal. Jared was enjoying a sleepover with Mercy and Honor's boys at Ada's house.

Debbie was grateful she wasn't alone. "Thank you all for being here. Joy, I know you never leave your children, so it means a lot that you're here tonight."

Joy gave her a huge smile. "We've had our problems, but everyone in this room has had problems with each other at some point. But we're always there for each other when needed."

Krystal didn't hold back her opinion, getting straight to the point. "He was never the one for you, Debbie."

Bliss could only shake her head in dismay. "Unbelievable, what he did. And writing a note? He should've had the courage to face you."

"I agree. He took the coward's way out. He's ruined his reputation," Favor said.

Debbie had held it together all day. "What's wrong with me? John insisted our marriage start off as a secret. Peter left me for Maisy. And now Fritz has left me for... for... no one. I must be an awful, unlovable person."

"You are a very loveable person. Their bad decisions had nothing to do with you. It's their loss," Cherish said.

All the girls murmured their agreement.

Debbie inhaled deeply. "For now, I'm only thinking a couple of hours ahead. It never works out for me when I try to plan long-term or even short-term. So, let's worry about who's sleeping where."

The room then turned into a whirlwind of makeshift beds from cushions and blankets. Amidst it all, Wilma made a sweet contribution, dropping off a bag of candy with a knowing smile before retreating.

Complaints of overeating clashed with the sound of candy wrappers. "I'm so full, but..." Cherish's protest was weak, even as she reached for a treat.

"Today, we can make an exception," Bliss agreed.

The rustle of wrappers filled the room. It was Krystal who broached the topic once again. "You know, Debbie," she started hesitantly, "when you're ready, there'll be someone who'll see just how special you are. Look at me. I gave up on love and had to get away. The last thing I was thinking about was finding someone else, and then I met Jed."

Bliss's nod was emphatic. "It comes when you're least expecting it. That's what happened for me, too."

"I can't picture it, not now... not ever again." Debbie shook her head.

"It's okay to feel that way," Honor reassured her, "but remember, not every man is Fritz."

"Your life is full, Debbie. With or without a man, you're loved," Mercy told her.

Tears threatened, but Debbie held them back. "I have Jared. He's enough."

With a playful gleam, Favor added, "And just think of the adventures ahead. Without Fritz, who knows what's waiting for you?"

The truth in those words resonated in the room. Debbie's eyes met each of her friends, seeing her own strength reflected in them.

"Debbie, just remember that everything that happens to you is *Gott's* will. You'll look back on this in a few years and you'll thank Him that this happened. I know it," Joy said.

"Maybe you're right," Debbie conceded, a hint of a smile warming her features. "I was so lost in Fritz's world... I forgot what it was like to think for myself. His family, his house, his decisions..."

"I didn't know that. Tell us more." Krystal leaned forward.

"Fritz always wanted things his way, and I... I was trying so hard to fit into his plans. Even the house we were going to live in wasn't my choice. And, I never did get along with his mother. Then there was his brother and Maisy."

"Let's see, so you never got along with his mother, his brother, or his brother's wife?" Joy asked.

"I got along with Fritz's brother for a time. We all know that. I got along with him until things went bad. I thought over time, things might change."

Bliss was quick to catch on. "You mean, you never felt at home with them?"

"Never, but I have Jared. What more could I want?" Debbie fought back tears. She didn't want to cry right now. Maybe she'd cry tomorrow.

Honor leaned forward and placed a hand over Debbie's. "Then it's a blessing. You're free to meet someone who values and fits with you better. He'll be like the last puzzle piece that will fit with you and Jared just right."

"And we'll make sure of it. We'll vet all your potential boyfriends," Bliss declared, igniting a round of laughter with her enthusiasm.

Debbie felt something within her start to shift, her pain receding a little. She scanned the room, her heart full with the people she had chosen as family.

"Maybe it is a blessing," Debbie whispered, almost to herself. "And perhaps this has made me stronger, and ready for anything."

Debbie's words ignited excited chatter as the names of potential suitors were playfully tossed into the air.

The night carried on, full of shared stories and whispered dreams. And amidst the comforting disorder, as the candles burned low, Debbie found a glimmer of peace, a whisper of change, and the promise of new beginnings. Beginnings that would be just right.

Eventually, the dark room quietened and all was still.

As Debbie closed her eyes, she anchored herself in this truth: she was not a casualty of fate or poor choices. With faith in God as her guide, she would embrace whatever tomorrow might bring.

Thank you for reading Whispers of Change.

THE NEXT BOOK IN THE SERIES

For a downloadable series reading order of all
Samantha Price's books, scan below or…

Head to SamanthaPriceAuthor.com

The next book in the series is:
Book 40 Her Hopeful Heart

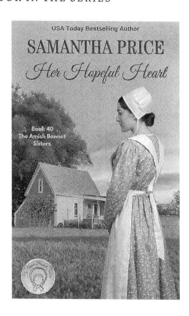

Debbie is stepping into a new life beyond what she had ever imagined, and her family is right there with her. They're pitching in, ensuring her new home is as warm and welcoming as possible. It's a team effort, and Favor and Cherish refuse to go home until it feels just right.

ABOUT SAMANTHA PRICE

Samantha Price is a USA Today bestselling and Kindle All Stars author of Amish romance books and cozy mysteries. She was raised Brethren and has a deep affinity for the Amish way of life, which she has explored extensively with over a decade of research. She is mother to two pampered rescue cats, and a very spoiled staffy with separation issues.

www.SamanthaPriceAuthor.com

instagram.com/samanthapriceauthor
pinterest.com/AmishRomance
youtube.com/@samanthapriceauthor